Ice Cold

Also by Andrea Maria Schenkel

The Murder Farm

Andrea Maria Schenkel

Ice
Cold

Translated from the German by Anthea Bell

Quercus

New York • London

Quercus

New York • London

ISBN 978-1-62365-720-8

Library of Congress Control Number: 2015937145

Distributed in the United States and Canada by
Hachette Book Group
1290 Avenue of the Americas
New York, NY 10104

Manufactured in the United States

10 9 8 7 6 5 4 3 2 1

www.quercus.com

Memorandum on the conclusion
of the trial of Josef Kalteis

SECRET REICH BUSINESS

The condemned man is not to be granted a reprieve. The sentence of execution is to be carried out in Stadelheim prison without delay. No public announcement is to be made.

Explanatory note: many crimes of this nature, dating from the beginning of the 1930s, are on the files. Such acts could thrive only on the barren ground of the Weimar Republic—democracy, that cancerous tumor, that breeding-ground of social misfits! However, the fact that, even after we took power, those crimes have not decreased in number, but continue to alarm and cause anxiety to our loyal National Comrades, is unacceptable. The National Community is healthy and must remain so in the future. Noxious parasites on the nation, like this man, ice cold in his crimes as in his very name, must therefore be removed from it. It is intolerable that such an anti-social character was able to prey on the western districts of Munich for years, soiling Munich itself, the cradle of the movement, the city so close to the heart of our beloved Führer.

Since the murderer is an ethnic German, an Aryan, and in addition a member of the National Socialist Workers' Party, immediate execution of the sentence and absolute silence are necessary. There is to be no announcement in organs of the German People's press such as the *Völkischer Beobachter*. For this reason all reports, both oral and written, are to remain strictly confidential. Any damage that might be done to the Party and the National Socialist movement is to be preempted. The appeal for clemency that has been lodged is rejected. Secure detention with reeducation in Dachau concentration camp is not to be considered either.

Heil Hitler!
Munich, October 29, 1939
Signed: . . .

*

He sits there. On the bed, his head in his hands. Eyes closed, open? He doesn't know. The room is faintly illuminated by the light falling in from the yard through the small barred window.

He sits there, he has been sitting there for hours. Always in the same position, hands folded as if in prayer, face half hidden in them, elbows propped on his thighs, motionless. Time passes. He feels as if it were running away through his fingers, along his arms, down his legs to the floor. Constantly. Incessantly. And yet however slowly it moves, he cannot remember anything. Not the day, the night, the hour, the minute . . . it is all blurred in that faint light, that endless gray, as if he too had dissolved, as if his life were already over.

Nothing is left, nothing, an endless space containing nothing, only a void.

Even fear has left his mind and his body. The fear that he was still able to feel yesterday. The fear slowly crawling up his back to his head, inch by inch. The fear holding his body, himself, captive. Lurking deep inside him, it numbed his thoughts and took possession of every single cell in his body, his whole being. Overnight, even that fear had given way to the void.

Hadn't been able to hold out, couldn't stand up to the void now filling him, taking him over.

At some point in the night the flap on the cell door is opened. Hearing the sound, he does not turn his head. Why would he? It means nothing anymore. Nothing means anything anymore. Nothing.

When the light in the cell is switched on again at six he doesn't notice it. Last night's wan, gray light still lingers around him. Head in his hands again, he stays sitting there on his bed. With the emptiness, with the void that is worse than fear.

He is still sitting like that when the two men enter the cell at around ten to seven.

They speak to him as they come in, but whatever they are saying he doesn't understand it. Words no longer penetrate this void, this vacuum all around him. Enveloping him, holding him in its grip.

He reacts only when he feels the touch, the hand on his shoulder. Knows it's time to stand up now. Slowly, mechanically, he gets to his feet. The men put his hands behind his back, and he feels the metal handcuffs on his wrists.

It takes him four steps to leave the cell. Four steps. He counts them.

The prison chaplain is already waiting for him at the cell door.

Whether he goes ahead of them or walks after them he cannot say, any more than he can remember the chaplain's words. He saw the chaplain open his mouth to speak. He remembers sounds trying to make their way to his ear. But they were disconnected, they made no sense. They didn't get through to him. Couldn't pass the wall of the void.

Once again he counts the steps. Every one of them, one, two, three, four . . . and then he hears the sound. The other sound, audible through his footsteps, urging itself more and more strongly on his conscious mind.

First quietly, then louder and louder, until it occupies his head entirely. It is the sound of the prison bell tolling for the last walk he will ever take. The death-knell. Its sound fills him now and his whole body.

Fills him as much as the void did before. He knows it will not fall silent until he is no longer alive. It will be the last thing he hears, it announces his death for everyone to hear.

He is brought down to the prison yard. They are already waiting for him there. The Public Prosecutor, the medical officer, and the executioner with his assistants.

Clad in black suits, the assistants receive him. They take him by both arms, one to his left, one to his right. Lay him down on his stomach on the tip board. He can still feel the firm grasp of their hands as they push the board under the guillotine.

The executioner pulls the locking lever. The blade falls, separates his head from his body.

*

The corpse, now the property of the state of Bavaria, is handed over to the City of Munich Institute of Forensic Medicine. The executed man's family has declined to claim the body, thus avoiding any responsibility for the expenses incurred. The fee of 247 Reichsmarks is paid to the executioner Johann Reichard from the funds of the Bavarian state treasury.

Duration of execution, from entry into the prison yard to death by the guillotine: 17 seconds.

SATURDAY

Kathie is sitting in the train to Munich. She has found a window seat, she's looking out. Raindrops patter on the panes. Driven by the airflow, they run across the windows in slanting lines, meet other raindrops, join them, merge into streets of rain. They're caught up against the frame, flow down the window in little streams. The landscape is hardly visible behind the wet window panes. The green of the meadows, the harvested fields, the forest, it's all blurred by the rain.

She sits there deep in thought. She's already far away from the village, far away in Munich. When they arrived they'd be going to Frau Lederer's. She and Maria. Frau Lederer is her mother's cousin. When she left home this morning she had promised her mother to do that, she'd had to promise. But as for staying, oh no, she wasn't going to stay there. Just leave her things and then go on. Why would she want to stay with Frau Lederer, who'd make the same rules as her father? Tell her what was right and wrong, decide on everything, her whole life. She wants to be free in Munich. Free. What about her promise? Well, she doesn't have to keep her promise, her mother will never know, and anyway Kathie kept her fingers crossed behind her back while she promised. And her mother didn't notice, so it was her own fault, wasn't it?

A few years ago, when Kathie was still a little girl, she went to Munich with her mother now and then. Not often. She was only occasionally allowed to go, and then she had to be a good girl. She had to sit by the window in the train like a good girl, hold her mother's hand like a good girl as they walked through the big city. Sit on the chair like a good girl and wait until her mother had finished making her purchases. So there sat little Kathie on chairs much too tall for her, swinging her small legs, waiting for her mother to be through with it at last, and then she'd get a special "town treat" for being a good girl. A bun with sugar on top, or a couple of sticks of rock candy.

Her mother bought fabric and all sorts of other items. Then she sold it on to the villagers at home in the country. She had her own little peddler's business. All the lovely things were stowed away in her big bags or the knapsack. Things from the city that you couldn't get out in the country, or if you could it was only with difficulty. Buttons, fabric, sewing silks, reels of cotton. And Kathie's mother sold a few kitchen pots and pans as well. Combs and ribbon bows, too. You could get such things from the nearest local shop, but even the nearest local shop was too far for many people to go, and "the Wolnzach lady," as they called Kathie's mother, would also take orders for this or that item and bring it back from town.

Kathie loved searching the bags for these delights, the colored buttons, the bows, the combs. Her mother didn't like her to do it. "That stuff is for sale," she said. But little Kathie often opened the boxes of buttons in secret. Looked at the treasures her mother brought home from the Munich stores.

Brightly colored buttons, mother-of-pearl buttons, Bakelite buttons. In every hue, red, blue, green. She even had silver buttons. Silver buttons that shone in the sun. Some like coins, others like little mirrors. She could gaze at it all for hours on end. The buttons, the sewing silks. It wasn't just ordinary thread her mother bought, no, she bought expensive sewing silk too. In all colors, to match the fabrics. Colored skeins of embroidery silks, patterns for the farmers' daughters so that they could embroider their trousseaux. So that the bridal carts would be full of linen when they left the parental home, and everyone could see what a girl was taking to her marriage with her.

Kathie watched to see just where her mother had placed the contents of the bags. She quickly put the boxes away when she heard her coming, put everything back in exactly the same place. Her mother mustn't notice that she'd been exploring the treasures again. Her heart was in her mouth, beating so hard that she was afraid her mother would hear it.

Once her mother brought a bead collar back from Munich. One of her customers had asked for it. These collars were the latest thing. You sewed them to your dresses. The glass beads were white, gray, and pink. Kathie held the collar in her hands. Felt the cool touch of the glass beads; the collar was so heavy lying there in her hands. She couldn't resist. With the collar around her neck, she examined herself in the mirror. She looked like a real little lady, she talked to herself in the mirror like one lady talking to another. Deep in conversation with herself, she didn't notice her mother. Never noticed her coming into the room. She was scared to bits when she heard her voice.

"Keep on looking at yourself in the mirror like that and one day the Devil himself will look back at you."

"How can the Devil look back at me out of the mirror?" Kathie asked.

"Just look in it long enough and you'll soon see. You wouldn't be the first it happened to. And give me that collar, it's not for you, I had to bring it back from Munich specially. It's for a customer, and she won't buy it if it's grubby."

Reluctantly, Kathie handed the collar back. Promised herself she'd have a collar like it herself someday, and not just one either. She'll look like the film actresses, the stars in the photos put up in the display case outside the cinema.

But Kathie still looks for the Devil in the mirror every day. She peers into every corner of it, in case she can see him, maybe even spot him looking over her shoulder. Beelzebub. She's never set eyes on him yet.

The Devil, the Devil, the Devil, the words are repeated over and over in her head, in time to the rattling wheels of the train. The Devil, the Devil, the Devil.

Maria, her companion on the way to Munich, sits opposite her. Eyes closed, tired out by the monotonous "chug-a-chug-a-chug" of the train, she's fallen asleep.

Kathie doesn't mind, she's glad of it. This way she can think her own thoughts undisturbed by Maria.

Dreaming of the job she'll look for in Munich, of her new life. She'll go to the Hofmanns, she wrote to them back in January. The Hofmanns know Kathie. Her mother always buys her fabric from them in Heysestrasse. And she's taken Kathie there too, to the place where they sell the fabrics, the buttons, the colored cotton reels. You only had to pick them up. Kathie still sees the cotton reel lying in her hand when she thinks of that. It was red, and she had closed her hand tightly over it. She didn't want to put it back. Nobody noticed her fingers closing around the cotton reel. The treasure well hidden in her little fist. Outside in the street, she showed her mother the reel of cotton.

"Stolen," her mother told Kathie. "You stole it. I can't take you to Munich with me anymore if you'll do a thing like that."

Kathie had to take her precious treasure back. Her mother propelled her into the shop ahead of her. Kathie can still feel the shame of it today, but Frau Hofmann didn't scold her, she just laughed and said, "I like the red ones best myself. Let's not take it so seriously, Frau Hertl, Kathie's only little."

She wrote to the Hofmann family asking if they could help her find a job in Munich. She wanted to work as a maid. Well, to start with. A maid in the household of a lawyer or artist or some other rich Munich family. She was sure the Hofmanns would help her, they must know such people. All the ladies came to buy from them. She's seen that for herself when she came to Munich with her mother, buying fabrics. The ladies with their hats and their furs. They all wore shoes with high heels and silk stockings. She wanted to own such things herself. She'd buy fine shoes and silk stockings. She'd buy them with the very first money she earned. She wanted to look like one of those city ladies.

The train stops on a clear stretch of line. Kathie looks out of the window. The rain is still running down it in large, heavy drops. The train slowly starts off again. Maria sleeps deeply; neither the jolting as the train stops nor the movement when it starts again can wake her.

Like Kathie, she plans to look for a job in Munich. Kathie is not pleased to have her tagging along. But she'll soon shake Maria off, she's sure of that. Once they're in Munich. Kathie looks out of the window again, this time there are no thoughts in her head. She just sits there and watches the raindrops following their course down the window.

Just before Munich, Maria wakes up at last. They help each other to get their cases down from the baggage net. Each girl has a small case with her. Not much. But the few possessions in Kathie's case are all she owns. She's put on her lovely green coat with the belt and the big green buttons especially for the journey, and her little blue hat with the pale ribbons, the hat she usually wears only to church on Sundays.

Gerda

February 18 was Carnival Saturday, that's the day of the Servants' Ball at Sedlmayer's inn. There's always plenty going on there, every year. The ballroom's very crowded. People come from all around. Well, it's the high point of the carnival season. You just have to be there. Of course I went too, what do you think? I danced and talked all night, and naturally I flirted a little bit too. With Franz. Franz used to be in service in Aubing, but he works in Munich now, in a factory.

What do they make there? Can't say, no, I don't really know. But he's pretty good at kissing, I can tell you that. That's why I was back so late, or more like so early.

He saw me to the front door and then he was off to the train station. On foot.

It was five in the morning when I went into the kitchen. How do I know so precisely? Well, I looked at the pendulum clock hanging in the corner of our kitchen. Right beside the sofa.

It plays "Germans To Arms!" every hour on the dot. So right at the very moment when I'm opening the kitchen door it's five a.m. and the clock strikes up "Germans To Arms!" I was so startled **I almost screeched out loud**. Stopped myself at the last minute. I didn't want Mother to wake up and notice I was only just home. I wouldn't have liked that.

I went over to the sink to wash. Icy it was, the water from the mains. The cold water really did me good. As I'm drying my face Mother comes in. She doesn't say anything, but she gives me kind of a funny look.

"Want a cup of coffee before you go to bed? I guess that'd do you good."

"Yes, thanks, Mother, that'd be just the thing."

"Anything special going on at Sedlmayer's, keeping you there so late?"

"Oh, it was crowded, and fun like always. And I met Franz and he saw me home."

"Ah, yes, that Franz. Working in Munich now, right? Come along, girl, sit down, coffee won't be a minute, and tell me what it was like over at Sedlmayer's!"

So I sat on the sofa and watched Mother making coffee. When it was ready she came over to me on the sofa with two mugs. She sat down and put the coffee on the table in front of us.

So we sat there talking. About the ball and who was there. And I started feeling sleepier all the time. I leaned up against Mother, and when I just couldn't stop yawning she said, "Time you had a bit of a lie-down. This is Sunday, your day off. You can miss church for once, the Lord God won't mind."

So I stood up and went to my room. I sat down on the bed, and just as I was beginning to unbutton my jacket I heard Mother calling.

"My word, take a look at that! Fine goings-on there must have been last night at Sedlmayer's! Lovers kissing right outside our garden fence, canoodling in the snow. Here, Magda! Look at this, will you?"

So I went back to my mother in the kitchen. If I hadn't seen it with my own eyes I'd never have believed it. Sure enough, there was a couple lying in the snow right by our garden fence.

"Well, imagine that! You'd think it'd be too cold for them, wouldn't you?"

Just then the man got to his feet. He buttoned up his coat, he looked around, and then he was off and away in the Aubing direction.

The girl—well, at first she just lay there. It wasn't until he was gone that she struggled up out of the snow.

I say girl, because now I could see she really was just a girl. Very young. She stood up and ran to our house.

"There's something wrong!" says Mother. Well, anyone could see there was something wrong.

So I buttoned up my jacket again, quick-like, got into my slippers, flung my coat on, and I was out of the house, wanting to see what was up. She ran right into my arms. What a state she was in! I put the hair back from her forehead, I looked into her face, then I saw it was little Gerda. The Meiers' foster-daughter.

So I say, "Gerda, what happened? What have you been up to?"

Then Gerda started crying.

"He grabbed my throat. He grabbed my throat, he pushed my skirt up and he pulled my panties off."

I could hardly make out what she was saying. She was all shook up, really shook up. Just kept on saying, "He grabbed my throat, took my panties off, pushed me down in the snow."

Mother, she came out of the house right after me, took the girl in her arms, hugged little Gerda tight. She was a picture of misery, Gerda was.

Like a little bird, I thought to myself. Gerda looked all ruffled up, like a little bird that's only just gotten away from the cat. That's how she looked when she let Mother take her into the house. Head hanging, shoulders slumped, she shook whenever she sobbed.

Mother held her arm tight, Mother just said, "Now you come along into the nice warm room. You'll be fine now. There's nothing to be ashamed of. Come along in and tell me all about it."

When I saw the state she was in, I was downright furious. So I jumped on my bike and rode after the man. I wasn't letting him get away, just like that. Not a fellow like him! I wasn't scared, I just felt so furiously angry. Very angry. So I got on my bike and went after him. I wanted to get on his track, I wasn't about to let him go.

I was just in time to see him disappear along the Aubing road. I cycled for all I was worth.

Up at Zacherl's, there was Frau Schreiber cycling along the road ahead of me. I pedaled even faster. I wanted to draw level with her, ask if she'd seen the man.

"No, there wasn't no one came this way. I'd have been bound to see him. Must have turned over there, in among the vegetable plots."

So I told Frau Schreiber—no, it was more like I shouted at her. "He's gone and attacked little Gerda!" I fair bellowed it. "That bastard attacked little Gerda!" And I was already turning toward the **gardens on my bike**.

I cycled along the path between the hedges, making for the **gardens**.

I couldn't see the man anywhere, but I spotted the gap in the fence. And the footsteps in the snow. I didn't see those until I got off the bike.

They led through the gap in the fence.

I stood there with my bike, didn't know what to do now. Couldn't make up my mind whether to push through the fence and leave the bike lying there. Luckily Frau Schreiber came up behind me. She was waving one arm around in the air. And shouting to me to wait for her. She didn't like to see me going after him on my own, so she'd turned her bike and followed.

Frau Schreiber saw the tracks in the snow too.

"He's through there. Must've got through the fence. This garden, it's old Frau Glas's," she said. "She's not here right now, she's over at her daughter's."

So I went into the garden through the gap in the fence, along with Frau Schreiber. We just left our bikes lying in the snow.

We found him behind the garden shed. Standing with his back to us. Looked like he was cleaning his coat, rubbing it down with snow.

He didn't hear us coming, because when Frau Schreiber spoke to him—what was he doing here, then?—he jumped. Looked at us quite scared, but then he pulled himself together, seeing there was only the two of us, and women at that.

"I'm not doing nothing here. Nothing."

He tried pushing past us. Shoving us aside with his shoulder, he wanted to push past. Try that on with Frau Schreiber and— well, he'd picked the wrong woman. She wasn't having any of that. She stood right there, hands on her hips, legs planted wide apart, that's how she stood. "You stop right where you are and tell me what you're doing here!" she barked at him.

"I'm not doing nothing. Nothing."

The man was almost a head taller than Frau Schreiber. He gave her a push, Frau Schreiber fell over backward in the snow, and he was off and away out of the garden plot.

He was running now, running like the Devil was after him. In the direction of Schmied's.

I was out of the garden plot next moment too. Back to my bicycle as fast as I could go, and I caught up with him at Zeiler's.

He was out of breath, couldn't hardly run anymore. I cycled along beside him for **quite a way**. I wasn't afraid, just angrier, and the further I cycled the angrier I grew.

He hissed at me, told me to back off. What did I want, he said, he hadn't done nothing. "Nothing! Nothing!"

I went on sitting on my bike, I never took my eyes off him. I was cycling along beside him all the time, very slowly.

"Don't be ridiculous!" I said. "I saw what you did. You just turn around and come to the police with me! They'll pick you up anyway! So don't be foolish, you come with me."

I was surprised at myself, I stayed so calm. I was trembling inside, but my voice was firm.

"I don't need you there. I'll go to the police myself."

"But I want to come with you. I want to see you go to the police. I saw what you did to that girl!"

"I know what I did. You let me be. I know what I'm doing. I'll go to the police."

When he said that, gasping with the effort, at that very moment I heard Frau Schreiber calling. She was coming along on her bike **quite a way behind us**.

So I turned around to her, and just for a moment I took my eyes off the man. And he saw at once I wasn't looking at him. He swerved like a hare and he ran for it before I could react. Past the Schmied property and over the meadows toward the next properties. All of a sudden he could run again. Me, I shouted as loud as ever I could.

"Stop! Stop! Help, he's getting away!"

I yelled at the top of my voice, and it brought Schmied running out of his place to see what the noise was. Why was I yelling like that? he asked. Was I out of my mind? he snapped.

I just shouted, "He's getting away! Stop that man, he knocked a girl over in the snow! You must stop him, for heaven's sake, stop him! He mustn't get away! He mustn't get away!"

And Schmied, he didn't stop to ask questions, he went haring across the fields after the fellow.

I just stood there with my bike. Just stood there in my slippers with my coat unbuttoned. Suddenly I was so cold, chilled to the bone, trembling all over.

And all of a sudden I was scared too, scared to death. I don't know which made me tremble most, my fear or the cold.

Because he could have pulled me off my bike. Pulled me off my bike and knocked me down myself. If that man had just taken a proper look at me, he'd have seen what a little half-pint I am.

Munich, February 28, 1939

Interrogation of Josef Kalteis
by Chief Public Prosecutor Dr. R.

Interrogation starts: 1030 hours
Interrogation ends: 1530 hours

—Josef Kalteis, I was born on the 26th of July 1906.
—In Aubing.
—Since December 31, 1937.
—My wife's name? Walburga, Walburga Pfafflinger.
—In Aubing. Number 2 Hauptstrasse, Aubing, that's where we live.
—For the Reich Railroad. I work as a switchman for Reich Railways.

—I trained as a mechanic, but I've worked for Reich
Railways as a switchman for four years now.

—Up till when my old works fired me, then I got this job
with Reich Railways. My dad helped me, he's with the
railway too.

—I work shifts, shunting the trains. We're on duty all
different times, that's how it is on shift work.

—What makes you ask a thing like that? What do you
mean, what kind of relationship do I have with my
wife? It's the way it is, that's all. What else would it be?
Sometimes OK, sometimes not so good, that's life.

—Well, we didn't hit it off so well at the start, not when
we was first married, but we get along better these
days. Better nor before.

—No, we didn't quarrel on Saturday. Has she said
we did?

—Yes, it's a fact, my wife did want to go to the movies.
But after she'd seen the trailer she suddenly wanted
to go home instead. Said she didn't like the movie after
all. She'd thought it would be different. Happens to her
quite often, she changes her mind a lot.

—What do you think I did? Took her home, that's what.
Didn't stay with her, though. I guess she'll have gone
to bed. Said she was tired, anyway. But I wasn't tired,
didn't want to go to bed yet, I put my coat on again
and went out. Over to Schmid's for a glass of beer. The
Schmid inn.

—I watched the card-players. The regulars playing cards
at their table. I guess I drank about three dark beers. I
met a man I know there, he could tell you it's like I say.

—His name? Can't remember his full name now. I
mean, I don't know him all that well. Just a guy I see

now and then. Exchange a few words with him, that's
all. No, I don't know his last name, I just know him as
Kurt. Kurt what? No idea. You'll have to ask the land-
lord at Schmid's.

—Then I went on to Huber's place with Kurt. The Huber
inn. Around midnight. Yes, I'm sure it was twelve midnight. At Huber's I met Adler. He was there at Huber's
when I came in.

—Adler, he works with me. The three of us went on
drinking.

—What did we drink, how much? Can't remember none
too well now. Two or three lagers it'll have been. Maybe
a schnapps or so as well. Adler wanted to go on to
Sedlmayer's. Very eager to go there, he was, said there's
always something going on at Sedlmayer's. And great
women there too, wow, real wild women, he said. So we
went on there, that'll have been about one.

—Adler was right. There was all sorts going on at Sedlmayer's. I drank ten or so shots of schnapps and a few
beers, three or four. Well, why not, when everyone's
having a good time? How much exactly? Can't remember no more. It was only on the way home I noticed I
was all boozed up, I mean drunk. But I saw Adler home
all the same. He couldn't hardly stand no more, let
alone walk. Hung on to me all the way, he did. I got him
to his front door. Over in Bienenheim, that's where he
lives. You just have to ask him. He'll bear me out.

—Then I didn't feel so good on the way back. All that
fresh air. I puked, had to crouch there in the snow for a
while, I felt so dizzy.

—Well, when I felt better, then I went on in toward Aubing. Wanted to get home. Lie down and sleep it off.

—Just before Aubing this girl crosses my path. She was carrying a milk can. She said good morning.

—I went along beside her for a bit. We talked. All perfectly harmless.

—A nice girl, she was. Real friendly.

—Yes, then I took hold of her.

—I put my hands around her neck and I pushed her down in the snow. Can't remember the rest of it. Only how I took hold of her around the neck and pushed her down in the snow.

—I can't remember no more. Why would I lie to you? I'd tell you if I could remember. You have to believe me. I'd put back a fair amount of liquor that evening. Sober I wouldn't never have grabbed her. Wouldn't be capable of it. I wouldn't never have done a thing like that. Never. I mean, I'm a married man. I got kids.

—If you say I tore her panties off, I guess that's right. But I can't remember for sure no more. Wasn't myself again until I'd finished.

—If she says so, I guess it's right that I . . . that I . . . well, that I rubbed against her. Oh God, oh God, I feel so ashamed.

(Puts his face in his hands.)

—I can't remember, just can't remember. Can't remember threatening her neither.

—It's the truth, I can't remember. I'm not telling you no lies! You have to believe me when I say so. You have to believe me . . .

(Begins weeping.)

Yes, yes, I'll calm down, I'll calm down right away.

(Takes the offered handkerchief, blows his nose.)

—*I can't remember nothing, not till I got up out of the snow and walked away.*
—Where was I going? Home, I was going home. Where else? Where else would I be going?
—Then these two women come after me on their bicycles. Wouldn't leave me be, those women. They kept on following me.
—Just before that I went into a garden. For a pee. And then they're suddenly standing behind me. One of them, I gave her a push, what else could I do? And the other, she kept going along beside me on her bike. Kept on telling me to turn myself in to the police. I couldn't get rid of her, couldn't shake her off. She wouldn't let me be. I couldn't even think no more. Not with all that yakking. I just wanted to get away. So I made off across the meadows, couldn't stand it no more. That's where the cops picked me up.
—There was this fat man who ran after me over the meadows. I don't remember if I shouted out I was going to shoot him. I suppose I could've. What was I to do? I was all turned around in my head. But I couldn't have shot him, could I? I mean, I didn't have no gun. I just said it so he'd clear out and leave me in peace. I wanted them to leave me in peace! In peace!
—You just have to believe me, I'd never have thought I'd do a thing like that. Attack a girl! Me? Never! I mean, I got kids. I'm a good dad to them! But I was so drunk that day. Didn't know if I was on my head

or my heels, I was so drunk. Lost control over myself.
You have to believe me. Do you believe that? Do you
believe me?

—I mean, I'd have turned myself in to the cops. When
I'd sobered up I'd have turned myself in. I'm not
a criminal!

—Oh God, yes, yes, I know I made a big mistake and I
can't understand myself, can't think what I was doing.
I mean, I got a wife and kids at home. I don't know
what happened inside me.

—No, I never did nothing like that before. I got nothing
to do with those other cases. Nothing at all! I wouldn't
have done such things nor even thought of doing them,
never in my life, what do you think?

—Yes, I've heard of cases around here. So's everyone
who lives in these parts. But I got nothing to do with
them. You can't pin that on me. You have to believe me,
I was so drunk, I'd never have done it sober, never. It
was a slip, just a slip! I mean, I got a wife and kids! I'm
a good father . . . I'm a good honest German citizen.

—Just because you've been looking for someone in these
parts for years . . . look, I know myself I did a stupid
thing, all that with the girl and so on, what I did, I
admit it, but I got nothing to do with them other cases,
nothing at all. Prove that I did, you'll have to prove
I did. Yes, just you prove it. Show me your evidence.
You won't find nothing! Nothing at all. I got nothing to
hide, nothing!

SUNDAY MORNING

Still half asleep, just on the point of waking up, she hears the voices. Far away at first, as if from the other end of a large hall. They grow louder and louder. The woman's voice is not unlike her mother's, hoarse, husky. Sounds from the kitchen, the clatter of crockery, now and then a small child whining. The sounds come closer, they're more distinct. Dragging her further from sleep and into wakefulness. Kathie opens her eyes. The room is small, the curtains closed. However, enough light falls into the room through the thin fabric to illuminate it softly. She lies there perfectly still, on her back. Only her eyes move over the room. Wander along the ceiling, down the walls, turn to the window. It's a small room, not much more than a cubby-hole. A wooden bedstead, a chest of drawers with a wash-basin and jug on it. The wardrobe stands in the corner next to the door. The air in the room smells musty, slightly moldy, damp. The walls are yellowed. Everything here is strange to her, for a moment she doesn't know where she is, how she comes to be here. Slowly, very slowly, memory returns.

Kathie sits up in her bed. She sees her clothes laid over the chair. The green coat, and over it her blue dress, her stockings. Just as she left them yesterday, before slipping into the clammy bed. She rubs her eyes, yawns. Knows where she is now, and how she came here the day before.

She remembers the journey by rail with Maria. Frau Lederer meeting the two girls at the station. She was standing on the platform when the train came in. Kathie knew who she was at once. Even before Frau Lederer herself spotted the girls. She was the spitting image of Maria's mother.

A brief handshake by way of welcome, nothing more.

She took the girls straight back from the Central Rail Station to Lothringerstrasse. They sat on the sofa in the combined kitchen and living room of her apartment, Maria beside Kathie. They drank a cup of tea. Kathie sat there quietly, silently looking around the room. It was a bright, spacious kitchen. The dresser was painted white, with curtains at the panes of the glass-fronted cupboards. A picture in memory of someone dead was stuck between the glass and the frame. A birdcage at the window with a canary in it. The canary was yellow, and Kathie couldn't take her eyes off it as Maria, beside her, talked and talked. Poured out words like a waterfall. Talked about her mother, Frau Lederer's sister, who'd had another baby in the summer. About her stepfather the farmer in Merl, the hop harvest, falling prices, the village people. Told Frau Lederer who'd been married, who'd fallen sick, who had died. Talked and talked. All the gossip she knew in full detail. Kathie was already sick of hearing those stories. The bird hopped from perch to perch in its cage, ruffled up its feathers, started preening itself.

Kathie looked away from the cage to Frau Lederer. She had an idea she wasn't very interested in Maria's chitchat either. Was tired of the girl's stories. But Maria never stopped talking.

Kathie sat there with her little blue hat on her head. The hat with its white ribbons. A tea-cup in her hand. She held it like a fine lady, between just her thumb and forefinger, crooking her little finger. She'd seen that in magazine pictures.

She dreamed her way over to the cage, through the window, out into the street. Dreamed of the city waiting for her, dreamed of her new life.

Frau Lederer asked if she'd like to take her hat off. Kathie shook her head. Didn't the ladies in the pictures always keep their hats on while they drank tea?

She drank hers. The taste of the tea was soft and sweet in her mouth, that was the sugar and milk in it. Sweet as the life she was going to lead here in Munich. In the big city.

She'd find a job and never go back to the country. It was much nicer here. She wanted to be a city lady. Luck lay about in the streets, she had only to bend down and pick it up.

"Where are you going to spend the night, Kathie?" asked Frau Lederer. Once again she tore Kathie brusquely out of her thoughts, brought her back to the kitchen and this table.

Frau Lederer had room only for her niece Maria. Maria could sleep on the sofa in the kitchen, but it wasn't big enough for two. Her spare room was rented to a lodger, she said, a gentleman.

"I know where to go. I'll go to someone I know in Ickstatt-strasse, Anna Bösl. I can stay with her," said the girl, a touch defiantly.

Did she know where Ickstattstrasse was, Frau Lederer asked? She, Frau Lederer, could ask her neighbor's girl to take her there. Frau Lederer herself was afraid she didn't have the time. So Kathie went to Ickstattstrasse. The neighbor's daughter and Maria took her there. She had left her case with Frau Lederer, she'd come to get it when she'd found a job. Later. Frau Lederer had no objection to that.

*

In Ickstattstrasse, Anna opened the door to the girls. She recognized Kathie at once. There were exclamations of "Hello there!" and "How are you?" and "Come along in. What are you doing in Munich? How long will you be staying?"

Such a warm welcome, very different from Frau Lederer's cool handshake. Kathie felt better at once. She said goodbye to Maria in the hall of the building, outside the apartment door.

A little later she was sitting at another kitchen table, this time with Anna. This kitchen was smaller and not so bright, but that didn't bother Kathie. And now she was the one who talked and talked. About the job she was going to look for in Munich, "because her father wanted her out of the house." But she'd have left anyway. The village was too small for her, she'd felt that for a long time. She was going to live in the big city. Like Anna. That's why she was here.

She hadn't been able to stay with her relatives, she didn't want to either, so now she was looking for a place to spend the night. Maybe Anna could help her.

"That won't be any problem. We'll soon fix it," Anna told Kathie. "You just have to wait till my mother comes home," she added, and she, Anna, would make sure that Kathie could stay here for a few days.

It wasn't long before Frau Bösl did come home. She looked tired. Kathie assumed she'd been at work. She sat down with them at the kitchen table, and Anna said, "This is Kathie from Wolnzach. I met her at the Merl farm, her and her mother. She's looking for a job in Munich and she needs a place to sleep. For now, just to start with. Later on she'll see."

Frau Bösl didn't like the idea of Kathie staying the night, and she didn't bother to conceal it. There was almost nowhere to sleep in the apartment, she said. She was renting the only spare room to Fräulein Stegmeier. And she was sure she didn't have to tell Anna how badly she needed the money since Anna's father died. Too much money to die on, too little to live on, it didn't stretch far enough anyway.

No, she couldn't let Kathie sleep in the bedroom either, because Frau Bösl herself slept there with her other two children, had Anna forgotten that?

"Fräulein Steigmeier's gone away for a few days. Couldn't you let Kathie stay here for the next few nights? Until she's found something else. She can't sleep in the street."

After some humming and hawing, Frau Bösl agreed, reluctantly, but all the same she said: very well, Kathie could sleep in the spare room.

"But only for the next day or so. After that she'll have to find somewhere else."

Didn't she have a case with her, asked Frau Bösl? She'd left it at Frau Lederer's, said Kathie. But Frau Bösl didn't seem interested in her answer. She rose from the table and went to the spare room. Opened the door and nodded in the direction of the doorway. "You can sleep in there."

But before that Kathie went out with Anna to the Soller inn on her first evening in Munich. To Soller's in the valley.

"Want to come along?" Anna had asked Kathie. It would be boring to stay here all evening with her mother, she added. Kathie was happy with that idea, so she went along with Anna to Soller's.

She met Mitzi Zimmermann that evening, and later on Hans too. Gretel, the waitress at Soller's, sat with them for a while, "Because there's not much going on here today, they're all out on the Wiesn for the Oktoberfest." She was curious, wanted to know who Anna's friend was, and Kathie told Gretel about herself.

Gradually the inn filled up with guests. Gretel rose to her feet and served them. Kathie and Anna hadn't been in the bar of the inn for long, maybe half an hour, when Mitzi Zimmermann came over to their table. Anna introduced Mitzi to Kathie. It seemed to Kathie that Anna knew everyone at Soller's, and everyone knew Anna.

A little later in the evening Hans arrived. Kathie liked him at once. As soon as he came through the door. With his gray felt hat, and his black mustache. He came over to their table. Mitzi jumped up at once and hugged him. Hans pushed her away when he saw Kathie. He wanted to know who she was, kissed her hand as if she were a fine lady. Kathie went quite red in the face when he looked at her with his dark eyes. He sat down on the empty chair beside her, moved really close, and Kathie liked that.

Where did she come from, he asked, and what was she doing in Munich? She told him all about it. All the ups and downs, the trouble with her father, and how she'd come to Munich to look for a job.

Finding a job wouldn't be easy, he told her, but he'd help her. After all, he knew plenty of people, and a pretty girl like Kathie was sure to find something.

"Oh, go on with you, don't talk such nonsense to the girl. You don't have any work yourself, like most who come here to Soller's, you live off Mitzi and the dole. As for the kind of work you have in mind for her, there's many young girls have come to grief that way."

"Don't talk such nonsense, just get on with your own job while you still have one." And Hans dismissed Gretel's objection with a scornful gesture.

*

It was a fun evening at Soller's. At some point Anna began to sing. All the street ballads that she and her father used to perform when she was little and they went about from inn to inn. And in the course of the evening Hans moved closer and closer to Kathie. He put his hand on her thigh. Kathie didn't push it away. Mitzi didn't notice, or if she did notice she didn't let it show.

Now Kathie slowly puts back the covers. They'd stayed late at Soller's, and it was well after midnight when Anna took her home to Ickstattstrasse.

Kathie was a little surprised that Anna herself didn't stay, just brought Kathie back to the apartment. Anna herself left again, but Kathie was too tired to wonder why. They'd fixed to meet again this evening and go to Soller's in the valley together. Anna would come for her.

Kathie pushes the covers right off, gets out of bed. She feels the cold floor under her bare feet. Goes to the wash-basin. What is she going to do until six o'clock, when Anna comes to get her?

She takes the jug, pours water into the basin, dips both hands in the cold water and washes her face.

Walburga

When exactly did I meet Josef? Can't remember now. We've known each other forever. Since we were kids. Over in the railwaymen's apartments on the housing estate, that's where we lived. My Dad's with the railway. Same as his too. Everyone there works on the railway. And they all have very many children. We kids, we always met to play in the yard. Mostly it was girls playing one game, boys playing another, but then with cops and robbers, that was different, we all mucked in together then. Boys too. That's how come I knew Josef. We were out of doors all day. Didn't go home until our Moms called us in, or the streetlights came on.

As a kid myself I always thought him a bit odd. When he was on our side he'd sit under the cherry tree, just sat there with his legs crossed, waggling them. Hardly ever said a word. Then sometime we kind of lost touch.

That was up till the summer of 1935.

That's when I met him again, bathing. Well, I really had a date to go bathing with Erich. I was walking out with him then, but did he care about me? Not him. Spent the time playing cards with his friends. Over on the benches by the kiosk. So suddenly Josef turns up, I see him standing there.

"Hello, remember me? I'm Josef," he said. I had to squint into the sunlight, so I didn't recognize him right away. Only when I looked closer.

Erich, he didn't have time for me anyway, so I just spent all afternoon talking to Josef. It was nice, but I didn't fall in love with him, no. He was kind of, well, like there, see?

He sat on the rug with me. Told me how he was working on the railways as a switchman. Just like his dad. Shift work. "So what do you do?" he asked. And I told him about my dress-maker's training, how I don't really like the job, but what else would I do? I'd need to be better at **math** to be a salesgirl in the Co-op or work in an office. So there wasn't much left, was there?

In the evening, he walked me home, pushing his bike. It was an old Dixi, with balloon tires. I remember it, yes.

The bike was stolen afterward, at least that's what he said. But that was much later. So he took me home, and when he made a date with me for the next Saturday I didn't say no.

And it was then it happened, I mean that Saturday. We'd gone out into the country, we went to Himmelreich on our bikes and when we were sitting on the grass he kissed me. It wasn't romantic, rough more like. But I didn't mind that. And then he wanted to go further, and I didn't say no then either. So well, that's when it happened.

I'm not very choosy that way, never was.

But when I never set eyes on him for several weeks afterward, well, that did annoy me. All the same, when he suddenly turned up one day I went to bed with him again.

"What've you been up to all this time?" I asked.

"Had a lot of work on," was all he said, and I couldn't get any more out of him.

I left it at that, didn't ask no more questions. I mean, the whole thing hadn't mattered to me all that much. Why would I want to ask more questions?

Then in autumn that year I found I was pregnant.

I'd hoped he'd take more care of me then, stick by me. But not him. Far from it. He didn't change his ways one bit, dropped in whenever he liked, then he neglected me and the baby too later. Hardly even looked at him. Let alone talking to the kid or playing with him.

And when the maintenance payments stopped one day, just like that, I went to the Child Benefit Office. My Mom and Dad had persuaded me that was what I ought to do. At the Child Benefit Office they had his wages seized. Well, I needed the money, didn't know what to do. Josef was angry, furious he was. That's the first time in my life I was real scared of him.

He was sitting on the bed in my room at my Mom and Dad's when I got home from work. Waiting for me. Beside himself, he was. Threatened me and called me names.

"How do I even know I'm the father? You could've just palmed the kid off on me."

I simply stood there crying. If my Dad hadn't come into the room, if he hadn't chucked Josef out of the place, well, I can't say what I'd have done.

So that looked like the end of it. "We'll bring the kid up between us all," my Dad said. So I didn't see no more of Josef for a few weeks. He never came next to or near me. And when I found I was pregnant again, it was me who went to see him. I just didn't know what else to do.

We married on December 31, 1937. It was snowing all day long. Why did I marry him? I'm not so sure myself. I guess I just wanted someone who'd pay for the baby, and I was more scared of being on my own than being married to a man I didn't love. I mean, who'd want me now, with one bastard kid and another on the way?

He agreed, said we'd get married. Didn't want no trouble with the Youth Office or the Benefit Office. He knew about all that from a friend of his in the Party. His friend had told him getting married was the simplest thing. For him, for all of us.

It was the Saturday three weeks after we got married he beat me for the first time. I can't remember what for, can't remember a thing about it. Except for the bash on the back of the neck he gave me. I'd just turned my back on him. I can still remember that all right. Then he grabbed me by the throat and pressed hard.

Seemed like forever before he let go of me again. After that I just wanted to get away, file for divorce and that. But the way he sat there, his face in his hands, telling me how sorry he was—well, I had to think of the children, poor little things, they needed their father, after all, and I stayed. I stayed against my better judgment, wouldn't listen to the voice inside me.

(Interrogation of Josef Kalteis, continued)

—My wife Walburga, she comes from the same place as I do, she's from Aubing too. Her old man is with Reich Railways, same as me.

—When exactly did I get to know her? Can't remember no more. She was in the same class as my sister at school, she lived in our neighborhood.

—One evening, I was at an inn, having a drink after work. So on my way home I see this girl in front of me. I kind of felt I knew her, so I walked a bit faster, wanted to see who it was. When I'd caught up with her I saw it was Walburga. I thought to myself, where's she off to, then?

—Yes, I was curious. So I went on following her. When I saw she was crying I spoke to her. I hate to see a woman crying. Never could abide it.

—Anything wrong, I asked her, what was the matter?
She told me to leave her alone.

But she didn't try to shake me off, I just went on
beside her. Well, I says to myself, you can't let the
girl alone now, not crying like that. So then she told
me about it, it was love troubles. How she'd been walking out with a man and she'd quarreled with him that
day. He was forever blowing hot and cold. That's why
she was crying.

—I went on walking with her for a while because I felt
sorry for her.

—I told her men aren't all the same, there's lots of
good fish in the sea. That made her laugh, because her
granny was always telling her the same.

—Then I saw her again a few weeks later, out bathing.

—I recognized her at once, and seeing she was all alone
again I sat down with her. And we talked all afternoon.

—I took her home, she didn't live far from me anyway.
And we made a date for next Sunday. Or maybe it was
the Saturday, can't remember now.

—We went out into the woods with our bikes.

—Then we went for a walk. After a while we stopped for
a rest, and she sat down beside me. Sitting on the grass.
I offered her one of my cigarettes, and we smoked.

—Yes, we talked. We was sitting there and, well, she
was the one who began necking.

—But I never did get much out of just necking. So I,
well, played around with her. She got wilder and wilder.
I had an idea she liked it, honest, so I just went on.
She didn't say nothing to stop me. Nor when I'd took
her panties off. She wound her legs around me. Wound
them around me good and tight. And she said ooh, that

felt so good. She started moaning. Well, kind of moaning and groaning. And she held me tighter with her legs. She was mad for it. Walburga was real wild. Oh yes, wild. I'd never been with a girl like that before. I enjoyed it. Honest, I enjoyed it.

—After that it was a few weeks before I saw her again.

—Not till she came to see me and said she'd gotten pregnant, then I saw her again.

—So we married when she was pregnant again. Last day of December, December 31, 1937.

—I asked around. I asked a fellow I know in the Party, and I asked at the Youth Office. They said it would be best to marry, seeing as I was the father of the children. I'd be better off that way. On account of the payments and that.

—With the first kid she went and got my wages seized because I hadn't paid up on the dot, and I didn't want no more of that. So then, well, I married her.

Walburga

He didn't come home from his shift till very late that morning, I remember that. Could've been around a quarter to five. It wasn't anything unusual, he was often very late home from work.

Not that I asked why. It was fine by me, him coming home so late.

His clothes were all dirty—"from work," that's what he told me. He undressed and washed at the kitchen sink. Then he sat down at the table to eat his breakfast. I'd made it by then, same as always. I mean, I knew what would happen once he'd finished his breakfast.

He'd grab hold of me by the wrist, haul me over to the kitchen table, or the sofa, or just push me up against the door. He'd hold me there with one hand, press the whole weight of his body up against me so as I couldn't hardly move, he'd grope under my nightie with the other hand. Spreading my legs, really rough-like. Push himself inside me without wasting no time. No feelings, no affection, so rough and violent **I was getting more and more scared**. Every time.

I'd close my eyes and keep still, didn't want to get him even more excited. There was times he let go of me, sudden-like, before he came. Then he'd tell me off for being so cold and not moving, no passion, he said, no wildness. He'd have to get his satisfaction somewhere else, he'd say, if he didn't like just getting himself off.

When he was in bed that day, September 30, 1938, it was, I plucked up all my courage and asked him for more housekeeping money.

The money simply wouldn't stretch, I said. He'd have to give me more if I was to get all those things. Even the monthly rent for our little apartment comes to twenty-five Reichsmarks, and then there was installments to pay on the furniture we'd bought, and the little boys had to eat too, they needed clothes. However careful I was with the housekeeping money, I said, however hard I watched every penny I spent, those twenty-five marks a week housekeeping just weren't enough.

All of a sudden he threw back the covers of the bed, shouting. Jumped right out of bed and went for me. I hadn't expected it. I mean, I didn't think he'd turn so violent. I just stood there. Couldn't hardly move a muscle. I stood there hearing him shouting and carrying on.

He never had a moment's peace in this place, he shouted, what more did I want, wasn't I satisfied with ruining his life already? Forcing him into a marriage he'd never wanted. And all because of that little bastard.

He kicked the crib where the baby was lying. He kept on kicking it and kicking it. It wasn't till then I managed to move again. I ran to the baby. To protect him.

That's when the blow hit me. He punched me right in the face. I hadn't seen him coming, just felt his fist punching my face, and the blood running slowly down my nose, all warm.

It wasn't till then the pain came. And my anger. The force of that blow had thrown me on the bed, I wanted to get up, I was trying to defend myself. But even before I was on my feet he hit me again. I fell back on the bed.

"Next time you can stay lying there, damn it. You won't move no more, you and your bastards!"

And with that he turned, put on clean clothes and went out of the house.

All this time I just sat there dumbstruck, watching him.

It was after that I packed up the bare necessities. Took the two screaming kids and left the place before he could get back.

I went to my parents with the children. That same day I went off to Munich on my own to file for divorce. I didn't care about the people on the train looking at me. Some of them kind of sideways, others staring straight at my swollen face. I couldn't hardly see out of my eyes.

(Interrogation of Josef Kalteis, continued)

—Me, hit my wife? I never hit my wife, never.

—Well, I may have given her a little push. Yes, I guess I gave her kind of a little push.

—I don't go hitting no women, if that's what she said— did she say that? Did she say I beat her? If she did it's a lie. It's a damn lie.

—She kept wanting more money off of me. Kept on and on nagging, wanting more, said she couldn't keep house with it. I mean, twenty-five Reichsmarks, anyone can get by on that, right? Twenty-five marks a week, that's plenty. But she was always wanting more. Money, money, money, more all the time! So I clocked her. Nagging like that, it got on my nerves. Well, so when I couldn't stand it no more I clocked her one. That's all. Just to make her shut up. Just to keep her quiet.

Walburga

It was late afternoon when I got back from Munich on the train. I'd been to that office where you file for divorce, and I did it. The fellow there was nice enough not to look straight in my beat-up face when he was filling out the forms. I was really grateful to him for that.

I had to go back to the apartment. I needed a few more things for the kids. And for me. Things I'd left behind, I'd had to leave them behind in the morning. I'd been so scared he might come straight back.

I didn't like to go into the apartment at once. Didn't dare. So I went to my Mom and Dad's place first. I waited there till I could be sure he was on the way to his night shift. Then I set off for the apartment. Late at night, it was.

There wasn't no light in the windows, the place was quiet. I'd waited outside the door for a bit, listening. I didn't want to run into him. It wasn't till I felt sure of myself I put the key in the keyhole and opened the door of the apartment.

Just for a split second all my fears came back. I was sure, certain sure, I'd double-locked the door when I left in the morning. And now I'd only had to turn the key very slightly. The door wasn't locked, it had just swung back on to the latch and snapped shut.

He'd been here during the day. Noticed I'd packed up some of my things, then he simply left the door unlocked behind him. There wasn't anyone in the place. I hesitated, then I went in.

Everything was dark, there wasn't no light except a little falling into the corridor from the stairwell. I didn't want to close the door. It felt safer that way.

The door to the bedroom was closed, like the door to the kitchen-living room. Suddenly the apartment didn't seem familiar anymore. It was threatening-like.

I stood there in the corridor, didn't know what to do, wanted to turn back. Hesitated. Made myself stay. Very carefully I opened the kitchen door. Didn't dare switch on the light in there. The room was dark, there was only the light from the street coming in through the window. The curtains wasn't drawn.

The kitchen looked like usual, nothing seemed different since I left it.

Everything was in its right place. Only the dresser drawer was open. I went over, took a look. Was there two knives missing? I couldn't be sure. Decided next moment not to think about it. Packed a few things up.

I had to go back into the bedroom, there was clothes I needed for me and the kids.

I looked around the kitchen one last time, then I left the room. Crossed the little corridor to the bedroom.

I slowly pressed the handle of the bedroom door down. Didn't want to make no noise. Opened the door just a crack at first. It creaked very slightly. I stood still, listening in the dark. Everything was quiet. I took a deep breath, pulled myself together and opened the door wide.

Just as I was feeling safe I heard that noise.

It was a soft hissing noise. You couldn't hardly hear it. But it came from inside the room. I was sure it came from inside the room, from the corner by the bedroom wardrobe. With only the open door and a few paces between me and it. I stopped, held my breath, didn't move a muscle.

I didn't dare go a step further. That sound, that weird sound had brought back all the fears I'd been controlling so carefully.

I slowly backed out of the room without so much as a squeal. Backed along the corridor. Never taking my eyes off the open bedroom door I reached for my bag. I'd left it beside the kitchen door. Still without a sound, listening for noises in the dark—oh, I felt that strung up—I snatched up the bag and made for the open front door, still walking backward.

It wasn't until I was in the stairwell that I turned around and ran down those stairs as fast as I could go. Ran on and on, all the way back to my parents' place. It wasn't till I was back there I calmed down and the fear ebbed away.

Then I didn't hear no more from him for weeks—weeks after I'd left the apartment on September 30. I was back in my old room at my Mom and Dad's, with the children. Then there he was all of a sudden, beginning of November. The doorbell rang, I opened the front door, and there he was in front of me.

He looked terrible, he said he was sorry for the whole thing.

I was to stop the divorce going through, he said, and come back home with the kids. "It won't do," that's what he said. And he wouldn't beat me no more, he'd promise me, he'd swear by the Holy Virgin. He'd swear never to beat me again.

I'll admit, I wasn't too sure at first. But the way he kept on at me, trying so hard to persuade me, well, I let him bring me around to the idea after all. I mean, I knew I couldn't stay in my old room at my parents' place for good, not with the two boys. And there was something I hadn't told anyone yet, I knew I was pregnant again. So I packed my things, put the boys in the handcart and went back to him and our old apartment.

Then I went and lost the baby a few weeks later. Can't say I was too sad about it. This way the poor little thing's been spared something, I comforted myself.

He fell sick early February this year, 1939. He was off work for the whole of the second week in February, hanging around at home, even had to stay in bed for a couple of days. He kept on at me, finding fault, didn't have a good word for me. The longer he was stuck in the apartment the worse it was for me.

There was no bearing it, he was so restless, worse and worse every day. Pacing around the apartment like a wild animal in its cage.

When I was just a little kid, my Dad brought a fox-cub home one day. He kept it in a little kennel down in the yard. It was very trusting. Then, when the fox got older, it kept on going up and down in its prison. Up and down, up and down, over and over again. It turned vicious and tried to bite. Until at last one day my Dad killed it.

I couldn't help thinking of that fox when I seen him pacing up and down in the apartment like that. Up and down, over and over again, like the fox. Getting more and more restless all the time.

If the kids didn't stay out of his way right away, he shouted at them. Kicked out at the little boys.

On Carnival Saturday he told he had to go out, nothing was going to keep him cooped up at home no more. He had to go out and find himself some fun.

I couldn't have cared less what he meant by that, I was sick and tired of his coarse talk and his hints. I hardly listened to him no more.

After that, I was very surprised when he said he'd go to the movies with me. He even went in, too. We watched the news-reel. Then we left before the main film. I was so tired, I didn't want to see it after all, and I didn't want to leave the kids alone so long neither.

It was a clear, cold winter night. I looked up at the stars, and the sky was sparkling away. We didn't go straight home, not the shortest way. We walked around for a bit because it was such a lovely evening. I was pleased he'd taken the time. I thought maybe everything might work between us yet.

We were home about nine-thirty. I was so tired, what with walking in the cold air, I undressed and went straight to bed.

He was off for a beer, he said, couldn't stand it here at home no more. He put his jacket and coat on again and went out. That's the last time I saw him.

SUNDAY

On Sunday morning, before church, old Frau Bösl puts a mug of malted coffee down in front of Kathie. "Here, drink that. You'll be on your own here all day. I'm going over to Haidhausen with the children after church to visit family. Our Anna will come for you."

So Kathie sits all alone at the kitchen table, drinks her coffee, indulges in her thoughts. She stands up, goes over to the window and looks out. For hours on end. When she just can't stand it anymore she goes into the bedroom and lies down on the bed, fully dressed. Closes her eyes and waits, waits for Anna to come to Ickstattstrasse and pick her up. And while she lies there she doesn't even notice she's getting more tired all the time, until the moment comes when she falls asleep.

In her dream, snowflakes are falling slowly from the black night sky. Little flakes dancing down, shining brightly. Kathie is a little girl again, she looks up at the sky, putting her head right back. Her woolly cap almost comes off. She sees the bright flakes falling, feels them cold on her face, she opens her mouth wide and tries to catch them in it as they fall, but they melt in the little girl's warm breath before they can touch her tongue.

Kathie reaches both her gloved hands out to the snowflakes. Sees them settle like stars on her woolen mittens. She feels the hand on her shoulder, large and heavy. Hears her grandmother's voice close to her ear, a hoarse whisper. "Come along, Kathie, we're going home now." She trudges home through the snow, holding her grandmother's hand.

At home she shares a room and a bed with the old woman. The bedroom is small and drafty, with only a thin partition to divide it from the rest of the attic. Frost-flowers made by their breath as they sleep grow on the window panes. On many stormy winner nights, small snowflakes fall through the poorly insulated roof. They fall in and settle on the wooden floorboards without melting. Those were the nights that Kathie liked, nights when she always lay very close to Grandma. Felt the old woman's warm body and closed her eyes, listened to the old lady's stories. Endless tales of ghosts and nightmarish specters, angels and wonders. She felt safe when her grand-mother's warm body was very close. Safe and warm, even now in her dream.

The old woman's body was bony in her old age. Bony from all the work she had done in a life of deprivation. Kathie's grandmother had borne ten children, all of them boys. She saw four of them grow up. The others died, some at birth, others before they learned to walk. Poverty was her constant compan-ion. Kathie's father was the first-born. He and his family lived in the little house now. The old woman moved into the attic room when the house passed on to him. Kathie had shared a bed with her as long as she could remember. She came into the world far too soon, did Kathie, premature, a poor little thing, she wasn't even as big as a beer-mug at birth, so the old lady told her. She took the little thing into bed with her and kept it warm, and so they went on. There were many nights when

Grandma coughed and gasped so badly that Kathie lay awake and couldn't drop off to sleep. All the same, she never wanted to move out of the room. She couldn't imagine, didn't want to imagine not sharing her bed with the old woman, the only member of Kathie's family who wasn't cold and forbidding. Her mother always out and about with her peddler's wares, her father angry and grumpy or coming home from the inn dead drunk. Those times he often fell down in the corridor and stayed there, sleeping it off. He'd sold off what little land belonged to the house, bit by bit, and drank or gambled the money away. If it hadn't been for the money from the peddler's trade, they'd have had to sell the little house itself long ago. They'd have been broke, as the old woman often said angrily, they'd have been hard up.

Kathie's grandmother warmed her, and Kathie felt good. But there were also nights when she was afraid of the old woman. Nights of full moon, when Kathie opened her eyes and the old woman's face was very close to hers. In the faint light and the shadows the old lady seemed to be staring at her, wide-eyed. With her gaze fixed on the girl. Moonlight falling in through the window had made the toothless old skull into something sinister. As if Grandma were asleep with her eyes open. Frightened, Kathie would sit there, staring at Grandma until she couldn't bear it anymore, and plucked up all her courage. She shook the old woman until she woke up, shook her with both hands. "Grandma, wake up!" she would cry. "Grandma, wake up, I'm scared of you!"

On one of those nights of full moon, she woke to see her grandmother sitting by the window. There she sat in only her nightie and her knitted bed jacket, staring at the moon. Kathie, curled up in bed and afraid, kept staring at the old woman and didn't know what to do. When she told her mother about it, Mama only said, "Let her be, she'll go back to bed when she feels cold. She's tough, she won't catch her death in a hurry."

But one December night death caught Grandma. It's four years ago now. Kathie slipped into bed with her. That evening the old woman's body seemed even bonier than usual. Kathie lay very close to her; it was an icy cold December night. A night of frost. Even as she fell asleep she heard her grandmother's cough, heard her heavy breathing rattle in her throat. It was almost morning when Kathie woke up. She felt cold, she'd been shivering, she put an arm out to Grandma, wanting to cuddle up to her. Only then did she realize how strangely cold and still her grandmother lay there in bed. She listened for her breathing, but however hard she strained her ears there was no sound to be heard. It was perfectly quiet in their bedroom. Kathie got out of bed and ran barefoot downstairs to her mother. And it was her mother who told her the old woman was dead. She doesn't remember what happened next, only that she saw her grandmother lying in her coffin in her best clothes. And that she, Kathie, had wondered why Grandma wasn't wearing any shoes. She wore her gray woolly socks in the coffin, but no shoes. In her black Sunday dress, hands folded over the rosary on her breast, she looked as if she were asleep. The gray woolly socks have stuck in Kathie's mind to this day, and she also remembers that she wanted to leave the village. Go away and lead another life, not the kind of life that Grandma had lived and the one that her mother was living.

And she feels hands on her shoulder again, feels as if they're large and heavy. She wakes with a start and doesn't see Anna until Anna speaks to her. It's already after three, and Kathie was fast asleep when Anna came into the room. She'd better get up quickly, Anna's in a hurry, she says, it's urgent. She wants to go and see Mitzi with Kathie, and after that to the Wiesn.

"It's silly to sit about indoors in this lovely weather."

Kathie is still sleepy, but glad to get out of the apartment all the same. She hasn't known what to do all day, alone in Munich like this. She puts her coat on quickly, and her shoes, and then they go over to Mitzi's on this fine, warm late summer's day. The air is mild, so she hasn't buttoned her coat up, she's left it open, she has her little blue hat on her head, she's strolling through Munich with Anna. To Mariahilfplatz, where Mitzi lives.

Kathie stops at every shop window they pass, looks in, just to see herself reflected in the panes in the sunlight. To see herself with her coat unbuttoned and the little blue hat on her head.

Mitzi lives next to the grocer's shop behind the church. The wording over the shop says Bombay Groceries. Kathie looks closely at the shop sign and reads it before they go into the building. Kathie likes Mitzi's apartment. It's light, and in the city center. As she sits there waiting for Mitzi to be ready, she looks around the apartment. Furnishes it in her mind. Decides she'll have a little apartment like this someday. She asks Mitzi how expensive an apartment like this is, and what kind of work does she do, to be able to afford such a pretty place?

Anna answers for Mitzi. "Mitzi here is an embroideress. But you can't afford a place like this just by doing embroidery. It's her fiancé who pays the rent. A fine gentleman from Gelsenkirchen. He has a little business and comes to Munich twice a year. Our Mitzi knows how to fix these things. You want to look for a fiancé too, you'll never afford a place like this working as a maid. You'd have to watch every penny. And here in Munich, well, Hans looks after her. You just have to keep your

eyes open and maybe you'll find someone to pay for an apartment for you too, someone to look after you. You'd have a pretty
good chance with Hans, and maybe something even better will
turn up." So saying, she winks at Mitzi and they both laugh.
But Kathie has got the point. Who knows, maybe something
would come of this apartment idea sooner or later? Anyway,
she's imagining herself in her own apartment. She'd have room
at last, not like at home.

"What are you looking like that for? Ooh, look, our Kathie's
miles away!" The voices and laughter have brought her out of
her thoughts. Back to Mitzi's kitchen at the table with the oil-
cloth cover. Anna is sitting on the chair opposite, still laughing at her. "Come on, get a move on, we're off to visit Mitzi's
sister Gustl in the hospital, and after that we're going to the
Wiesn."

So they set off, Anna, Kathie and Mitzi, on their way to
Thalkirchnerstrasse.

It says DERMATOLOGY on the door of the hospital department.
Kathie has no idea what that means, she just follows the other
two into the ward where Gustl is lying. There are six of them
in the ward. The separate beds are divided from each other by
curtains, most of them not drawn. The curtain around Gustl's
bed is open too. Mitzi's sister lies in bed, very sick. She looks
white, almost translucent, and weak. Her hair is thin and sparse
although she's still a young woman. Kathie thinks she can't
even be in her midtwenties, although she has an old woman's
face. She complains of the hospital food. And the strictness of
the nursing nuns, they treat you like dirt, those preachy ladies,
as Gustl disparagingly calls them. Mitzi secretly slips her a few
cigarettes, asks when she can come again, that's if Gustl would
like her to, and then visiting hours are over. Kathie is glad to

get out of the hospital into the open again, the air in that ward almost stifled her.

They go straight from Thalkirchnerstrasse to the Wiesn, and it's an even nicer afternoon there. They're in the beer tent, where they meet a few fellows who invited them to have a bite to eat, and they go on the swingboats and to the shooting ranges too.

It must be about seven when they arrive at the Soller inn with their companions. It's at Soller's that Anna tells her the story of Mitzi's sister. How Gustl had been going out with an artist. A well-known artist here in Munich. Gustl had been very pretty, not the picture of misery she is today. She worked as an artist's model, or as she was always saying his Muse. Anna twisted her lips and sounded sarcastic as she uttered the word "Muse." They really lived it up at the parties that fine gentleman gave. Or at least, that's what Gustl told Mitzi. Anna was ready to believe those stories, though she'd never been to the parties, but she'd heard things. Mitzi had told her about the parties, and she, Mitzi, had it from her sister. Gustl never showed her face here at Soller's. Why would she want to come to a place like this? She moved in very different circles. And those fine artists, they were partying all the time. Seems the bubbly flowed freely at those parties. Seems they had money and to spare. Not like the poor starving fools here at Soller's. As for that artist of Gustl's, he was very peculiar. Used to go around stark naked wearing just a feather.

"Just a feather, think of that, and guess where he wore it? Up his ass! Up his ass! Really perverted, seems he wore feathers in his ass like a peacock. Well, that's what Mitzi says, but he paid well. He always put the money under the bedspread. Only coins. That's what those artists are like, they think up funny ideas, they don't just put the cash down for you. He used to count it out coin by coin in the bed, put the sheet over it, and Mitzi's sister had to lie on top of it. Acting as if she didn't know her fee was under the sheet. That got him tremendously excited, and afterward, when she counted the money, he wanted to watch that too. Well, everyone has their funny little ways. They lived it up, they really did. She was always laughing at us, she had money, and he took her traveling with him—until she caught syphilis. Poor thing. There she is in Thalkirchen, in the Dermatology department. You saw what she looks like now. Her hair's all fallen out, she looks like an old woman. That artist had other Muses too, and guess how quickly his prick drooped! He dumped her just like that. No more feathers, no more bubbly."

Hans is at the Soller's too, he thinks it's a very funny story. Says he guesses "that artist fellow thought himself cock of the walk," and Hans crows like a rooster, again and again. They laugh, Hans, Anna and Kathie, laugh until the tears run down their cheeks.

But in the course of the evening they forget all about the story. A blond man comes into Soller's and sits down by Kathie, asking if the place next to her is free. Kathie doesn't say no. She likes the blond man, she makes eyes at him, and he smiles at her. Is she new here? He's never seen her here before, though he come to Soller's almost every day. He teases her, and as she's hungry she lets him buy her a meal; after all, she's had nothing hot to eat all day, only that snack on the Wiesn and a mug of coffee.

Around midnight Anna leaves, and Kathie goes with her. The blond man accompanies them for a bit, says he's going their way. So they all arrive back in Ickstattstrasse together.

Kuni

I remember the day I met the girl very clearly. It was September 29, 1938. A Thursday. The day when Mussolini came to Munich. Not a thing I'd be likely to forget. My wife wanted to go into town, see the Duce. "You don't get to see him every day, and with a bit of luck we'll see him driving toward the Feldherrenhalle in the open car." My Lisbeth was wild about the Duce, said she absolutely had to see him. "Such a fine-looking man." I'd have liked to go into town with her too, but I couldn't. That was the day I had to stand in for my friend Zimmermann. Zimmermann was due to give a talk to the people on the air-raid precautions course. He'd been an ambulance man in the war, same as me. But then he was sick for a while, so I stepped in for him. My Lisbeth was a bit upset because I couldn't go with her, but still, she went to town on her own. By train, in the morning. There were one or two things she had to do, she was going to meet her cousin and then spend the evening with her, just in case it all went on late. I had the day off because originally I'd been going to Munich too. And I still had some vacation time due to me, so the trip to Munich would have been a nice idea.

The 29th was another lovely summer's day, and I didn't want to spend my day off sitting around at home on my own. I went for a bike ride in the morning. First I went to the station with my Lisbeth, and then I went straight on to Hohenpeissenberg to see an old friend who used to work with me. It's a nice ride from where we live, just right for a day's outing.

I spent the day with my old friend. He's retired already, his wife died not long ago, so mostly he's alone. That's the way the world goes. We went into the garden and drank coffee there, because like I said, it was lovely weather that day. His daughter, she lives nearby, she'd baked a cake with plum topping specially. We had a good time. It'll have been around four in the afternoon when I went home. I had to go to the air-raid precautions course in the evening and give that talk, and I wanted to look through the notes Zimmermann had given me first.

So I cycled back to Peissenberg along the main road. It must have been around mile marker 50 when I saw the woman. She was lying there a few yards ahead of me, right on top of the tree-trunks stacked to the right of the carriageway. I didn't even have to get off my bike to see the girl was completely exhausted.

I know about these things, you see, I was in an ambulance unit in the war, so I can judge that kind of condition. I don't know how many people I saw at the time, exhausted like that. Must have been dozens if not hundreds.

The girl's bicycle was lying at the side of the road next to her. At least, I assumed it was hers, because there wasn't another soul in sight anywhere. There was a cardboard box on the carrier of the bike. I'd say it was about 18 by 12 inches. I remember that cardboard box because I was surprised it hadn't slipped off the carrier when she let the bike fall in the grass. Can't remember what color it was now, no, only seeing the box still there on the carrier.

So I got off my own bicycle and went over to the girl. "Can I help you?" I asked her. "Are you feeling ill? Is there anything I can do for you?" She said, "No, thank you, everything's all right, I just feel so terribly tired."

I asked if she'd fallen off her bike or had an accident. But she wouldn't accept any help. "No, thanks, I'm fine, just so, so tired," she repeated.

Well, what would you have done? I wasn't going to leave the girl alone there, I couldn't, not with her in that state. So I asked where she'd come from.

"Steingarden."

Had she come straight from Steingarden? "No, from Füssen," she told me.

"For heaven's sake, you must already have cycled nearly 35 miles today. Where were you headed?"

"Starnberg."

"You can't possibly get there, not in your present state. It's another 18 miles or so from here to Starnberg, maybe 35. You must drink something. Do you have anything to drink with you?"

"No."

"Well, you have to drink something, child, and have a bite to eat too. A little thing like you!"

I mean, tell me honestly, how could I leave her alone in that state? Not the way she was, there at the side of the road. So I persuaded her to let me go with her part of the way. I picked her bicycle up, and we pushed the bikes along side by side. I wouldn't let her ride hers, she was so exhausted. So I took the short cut through the woods with her. By the time we came out again on the old state highway, she was strong enough to get on her bike again. We cycled on together to Peissenberg.

On the way I talked to her. She told me she was going to look for a job in Munich. Her home was in Unterellegg, near Sonthofen in the Allgäu. She had a sister in Munich, she said, a married sister who lived in Sendling, and another sister who had moved to Munich quite recently and was getting married soon. She was going to visit both her sisters, and she was taking the bicycle to one of them, because it really belonged to her, the sister. That's why she was traveling by bike and not on the train, on account of taking the bike to her sister in Munich. And she wanted to go to her younger sister's wedding. Her mother was coming to the wedding in Munich as well, and they'd meet up there.

When I said it would have been more sensible to come by train and take the bicycle as luggage, all she said was, "I can't afford the train, by myself or with the bike. I'd have had to borrow the money. Anyway, I cycled to Munich once before, so it came in really useful that I could go on my sister's bike. If only that horrible man hadn't followed me on his bicycle at Steingarden, I wouldn't have been all out of breath like that. He rode along beside me all the time, and he kept trying to look under my skirt. I was scared he might pull me off my bike. I'm not having any of that, I thought, and I cycled like crazy until I was sure he wasn't following me anymore."

So finally, when we reached Peissenberg, I said she could come home with me, freshen up a bit and stay the night if she liked. It would surely be better for her to get some rest, I said. But she refused, she said she really had to cycle on to Starnberg today.

I felt sorry for her, so I gave her ten pfennigs for something from the bakery. "Since it seems that's all I can do for you," I told her. She was glad to accept the ten-pfennig piece. She went into the shop, and I waited outside with the bikes. When she came out, she asked me if I could lend her a little more money, she'd like to buy some sausage from the butcher's shop too. So I gave her another 35 pfennigs for some sliced cold meat. She said she'd never met anyone as kind as me, she didn't know how to thank me. I asked her again if she wouldn't change her mind.

"The offer's still open," I said, "you could stay the night with me." But she shook her head again and said no, she really did want to go on. She'd easily do the 22 miles now she'd had something to eat.

So we went on a little further together, and I said goodbye to her outside my place. I stood outside the door for a while, watching her cycle off. Then I went indoors. It must have been nearly six o'clock, and I had to look through the notes for my talk. It was getting late.

What did she look like? All I know for sure is she was wearing a green raincoat and a dirndl dress. Her hair? Oh, her hair was bobbed, know what I mean? It suited her thin face. All things considered I'd say she was a pretty girl.

*

It was getting late now. She didn't remember Munich being quite such a long way off. When she cycled there five years ago, the same stretch of road had seemed far shorter. Had she been wrong? And she hadn't been nearly as tired and exhausted as she was today. Of course, if that man in Steingarden hadn't followed her she could have managed her strength out much better. But she'd cycled as if the Devil himself were after her, and just before reaching Peissenberg she simply couldn't go on. Everything went black in front of her eyes, and she found it hard to catch her breath. Her lungs were short of air. She hadn't eaten all day either. She was exhausted, so she sat down on the tree-trunks at the side of the road in the sunlight. But after a while even sitting was too tiring, so she simply lay down. She very nearly fell asleep, she was so tired, she'd closed her eyes and was listening to her own breathing.

She'd slept at her auntie's in Füssen last night. She cycled away right after breakfast, at four in the morning. She'd borrowed two marks for the journey, but in the end she didn't buy anything to eat with the money.

Lying there like that, gradually getting her breath back, she never noticed the man. And when he spoke to her so suddenly and unexpectedly she was really alarmed at first. He was getting on in years a bit, he wore plus-fours. He asked in a kind, attentive way if there was anything wrong, had she had an accident, did she need his help, all that soft soap. At first she wished he'd simply go away and leave her alone. But then she remembered the horrible man in Steingarden, and she was glad he was there and would go with her part of the way.

At least, she was glad of it at first, but when he insisted on taking the short cut because she was still so tired from cycling, and he told her how his wife was away all day and spending the night in Munich "with her cousin, on account of seeing Mussolini," she felt he was pestering her a little. He kept coming closer, then he put his arm around her shoulders as if by chance, even his voice suddenly sounded over-familiar. He seemed a little weird to her, a little strange. She was relieved when they reached the road and she could get on her bike at last.

She let him buy her something to eat in Peissenberg. Why not? That way she could save her two marks. But when he repeated his invitation for her to stay with him overnight, she refused again. Never mind how thoughtful he sounded— "But my child, you're still worn out!" and "I just can't let you go on in that state, my child!" All that "my child" business, it got on her nerves. Why didn't he say straight out what he wanted? She wasn't a child anymore.

No, she most certainly was not, she had a child of her own; that's what came of walking out with Heinrich. The little boy was three years old now. Heinrich had been a dead loss. Hadn't paid a penny of maintenance, didn't even intend to. But to be honest, he couldn't have paid anyway. He'd been a deadbeat, no use to anyone. Always shooting his mouth off, nothing behind his fine talk. The last she'd heard of him, he was in jail. They arrested him for something or other, exactly what she didn't know, didn't care either. She found a foster family for the little boy. What would she do with a child when she didn't even have enough money for herself? She was going to look for a job in Munich. She'd tried that once before, five years ago, she'd spent a couple of weeks there. But times had been much worse then than they were these days. She'd heard it was easier now, and with the reference Dr. Kaiser had given her she was sure she'd find a job as a maid in Munich. She was certain she would. She had a nice feeling that everything in her life was about to change for the better.

She'd thought just now it would be a good idea to find somewhere to sleep. She was tired. Her legs felt so heavy. She'd almost stopped at the last inn she passed to ask for a bed for the night, spending the last of her money on a night's rest. But then she changed her mind at the last minute and cycled on. She'd get there today, she was sure she would. It wouldn't be far from Oderling, she'd soon have reached her journey's end. It wouldn't be far now.

*

My name is Regina Adlhoch, I live in Unterellegg in the Wertach area.

My late husband was a farmer. I live on the farm with my son, it's his now, and my daughter-in-law.

I came here because my daughter Kuni is missing. Kunigunde Adlhoch, that's her full name.

Kuni was born on August 21, 1915, in Unterellegg.

I last saw her on September 28, 1938.

Up till the beginning of September Kuni was still working for Dr. Kaiser in Freiburg. I can't tell you why she left her job there, I don't know. She didn't tell me anything about it. She came out to the farm and stayed three weeks. She slept with me in the little annex I moved into when my son inherited the farm. I don't think things were going well for her, because she always came home to me when things weren't going well.

After three weeks she said she'd be off again. I didn't ask her any questions, I didn't want to. So she set off on September 28 early in the morning on the bike, to go to our relatives in Füssen. She slept there on the night of the 28th. The family there told me she got up early on the 29th and set out on the bike again for Munich.

She said she was going to look for a job in Munich.

Usually I hear from Kuni every three or four weeks. But it's nearly three months since she left now, and I haven't had a word from her. I'm very worried, I've always heard from her before. Always.

The bicycle she had with her—well, she was really taking it to her sister in Munich. That's what they agreed, but she never turned up there either.

I was in Munich myself early in October. I went by train. Resi, that's one of my other daughters, was getting married there. She's married a really nice man. I'd hoped Kuni would go to Resi's wedding. She might wander here, there and everywhere in the usual way, but she'd go to see her sister. That's why I was so surprised that Kuni didn't turn up for the wedding. It was all agreed.

It's not the first time Kuni simply went off. She was in Munich once before, five years ago. She wanted to look for a job there. She didn't say anything about it that time either, and I didn't hear anything from her. But she was back home with us again four weeks later. Kuni always came home again after a few weeks.

I'm afraid I have to say she's rather flighty. But she has a good heart, even if she never stays anywhere long. However, she's never been away from home so long before without me hearing anything from her.

I'm so worried about the child, that's why I came, I want to report her missing. So that you'll look for her and maybe, God willing, you'll find her.

(Interrogation of Josef Kalteis, continued)

—The day Mussolini came to Munich I was out at the Kiefern inn in Obermenzing, killing a pig.

—That's right, I helped with the pig-killing. I've often been over there to help out before.

—You want to know what I did there? Oh, I can tell you that all right, I can tell you all the details.

—The butcher kills the pigs in Obermenzing, he always asks if I can come and lend a hand. I like it. When you're taking a sow to be slaughtered she knows what's up, I can tell you. That's when they start screaming. They start screaming out loud the moment you fetch 'em out of the sty.

—You need a couple of men to hold that sow or she'll make off. You have to brace yourself against her. So as she won't make off. You have to brace your whole weight against her, good and hard.

—You feel the sow twisting and turning, trying to get away. You hear the fear in her grunting, the fear of

death. You see her rolling her eyes in terror. She's so
scared, that sow, she foams at the mouth.

—You tie the back leg with a rope. You put it around
the leg and tie it tight, or she'll break free. Then
along comes the butcher, brings his hatchet down on
her head.

—With the handle, I mean, not the blade. That's how he
does it! Boing!

(Kalteis swings his arm back and shows those present
how the butcher hits the pig.)

—Boing! Mostly he has to hit her twice. First time
around the sow is just left dizzy, half- stunned. Second
time her feet go from under her. Crash!

—You feel the sow collapsing, you feel her knees give
way. Then the butcher slits the sow's throat with
his knife.

—Through the vein right here. Then you catch the
blood in a basin. It's got to be stirred to keep it from
clotting, see? You stir it for five minutes or so till it's
cooling down.

—That's the part I like best, stirring the blood. That's
my job! I really like it.

—Next you have to scald the sow with hot water so as
to shave the bristles off better. You shave the bristles
off of the rind, you want that sow good and clean.

—Everyone has to lend a hand there. You need hot
water and pitch, then the bristles come off easier. You
put the sow in a trough, it's a wooden trough, pour the
pitch over her and the hot water. It has to be almost
boiling when you scald her. If you don't have no pitch

and hot water, well, it's a pig of a job, you might
say. Can't be done, I've tried, you can only scrape a
little bit of skin clear with a knife. Can't do no more
nor that.

—Then you lift the sow out of the trough. A sow like
that, she'll weigh just under three hundred pounds. You
put the carcass on a ladder and rub the back and the
sides down with a chain. Chains is the best way to get
the bristles out. And what won't come out you scrape
off with the knife.

—Then you hang the sow up. By her back legs, head
down. Like she's hanging on the gallows. You stick the
knife in and cut the sow apart from top to bottom.

(Kalteis shows those present how it is done.)

—*Then all the innards drop out. You have to be careful
not to slit the gut or the shit will all fall out. A filthy
mess that makes.*
—After that you wash out the gut, you'll be needing it
later for sausage-skins. I mean, you stuff the sausage-
meat into it. I don't like washing out the gut half so
much. I'd rather stir the blood or help cutting up
the sow.
—When she's cleaned out you chop her apart down the
middle with the hatchet. And then you cut up
the halves.
—For the hams you put the knife in on the inside. Here,
this is where the knife goes in.

(Pointing to his thigh, Kalteis shows those present
where and how he uses the knife in butchering a pig.)

—Right here, this here is where the knife goes in. Stick it in further down and you'll miss the joint. You can't get the ham off whole, not without you find the joint. You have to cut all the way around once. It's not as tricky as it looks, not if you know the right place. That way you soon have a ham, but you have to find the right spot. The sinews aren't no problem, you've cut 'em through already.

—But it gets tricky if you don't go for the right place, on account of you can't cut through the bone. If you've cut all around it first, the ham turns on its joint easily.

—Yes, sure it's hard work, you work up a good sweat, but once you know how to do the job, it's real easy.

MONDAY

When Kathie gets up and goes into the kitchen at nine in the morning on Monday, old Frau Bösl is standing at the stove, and Anna is sitting at the table in her mother's kitchen. It looks as if she's been waiting for Kathie.

Kathie sits down at the table with her. "Well, so madam's out of bed at last, is she?" says Anna to Kathie. "We weren't all that late at Soller's!" Laughing and winking at her. "Or was it such hard work necking with that blond fellow?"

Old Frau Bösl pushes the mug of malted coffee and a piece of bread across the table to Kathie. "Here you are, have something to eat and drink." As she pushes the mug over, coffee slops out on the tablecloth. Kathie takes the bread and crumbles it into the mug. She watches the bits of bread slowly soaking up the hot liquid. Then she fishes them out with the spoon Frau Bösl put ready for her, piece by piece. Anna sits opposite the whole time, watching Kathie have her breakfast.

"Going to be much longer? I don't have forever, you know." Anna's on the dole, has to go to the office to pick up her thirty marks, and she has something to discuss with Kathie too. Anna is in a hurry, they start out immediately after breakfast. Kathie just has time to get her coat and her bag.

On the way Anna tells Kathie she'll have to find somewhere else to sleep. Her mother doesn't want her sleeping in the apartment anymore, the lodger Fräulein Stegmeier comes back today, and she pays well for her room. Anna's mother needs the money, her widow's pension is small because her father paid for hardly any insurance stamps, and she can't pay her rent with just the tiny pension and what she earns as a washerwoman.

Kathie goes along beside Anna, can hardly keep up with her. Doesn't know what to do, where to go. She can't sleep at Frau Lederer's, she wouldn't want to. Anyway, Maria was there, and now there wasn't room for her at old Frau Bösl's either. She'd said all along she couldn't stay more than two nights, but where was Kathie to go now? She wants to ask Anna, "How about your place?" But as if Anna could read her thoughts, she answers Kathie without being asked.

"You can't sleep with me, I'm sleeping on the sofa at Mitzi's anyway because I don't have a place of my own, not since Lukas chucked me out, that's my fiancé, the bastard. Mitzi's all right, *her* fiancé, the one in Gelsenkirchen, he pays for the apartment. You could do with luck like that, right? One man to pay for your place and keep you, another to suit your desire. That'd be just the thing! You can always go to the hostel, the Marienherberge. Do you have two marks?"

Kathie, walking along beside Anna in silence, nods. Yes, she has two marks.

"Then you'll have a place to sleep, and if you don't like it there, well, you're a nice clean girl, look for a man of your own. That blond guy, he seemed taken with you. Then you'd have a place to sleep until you find something better. Hey, don't look like that, only joking!"

They go to the Marienherberge in Goethestrasse together, and Kathie registers at the hostel. She is told to come back in the evening and she'll be given a bed. But not too late, she'll have to be there around seven or eight in the evening at the latest, if she wants a good place. She'll get a hot breakfast next day too, but then she must leave the hostel. No one's allowed there during the day.

Suppose she finds somewhere else to sleep after all, Kathie asks the hostel manager, then what?

"If you don't turn up, then you forfeit your money. We don't refund it. And don't forget you'll have to be here by ten, or all the beds will be gone."

Kathie takes the two marks out of her purse and puts them on the table. She has to sign in the register beside her name and then she can go. She walks around the city with Anna for a bit, until Anna leaves her, saying she has things to do. She doesn't tell Kathie what they are, and Kathie doesn't ask.

So Kathie goes on strolling through Munich on her own. Seeing the city, looking in the shop windows, just wandering aimlessly around the streets. At some point that day she finds herself in Heysestrasse outside the Hofmann family's shop. How she came to be in Heysestrasse she doesn't know, she was just walking nowhere in particular. She hesitates for a while, wondering whether to go in or not. But it can't hurt. So in she goes.

Inside the shop everything still looks just the way she remembers it. Frau Hofmann is standing behind the counter as she always did, and Kathie goes straight up to her. "I'm Kathie, Frau Hertl's daughter from Wolnzach," she introduces herself. For a moment Frau Hofmann looks blank, then she remembers Kathie. "Oh, my God, so it is! Kathie who likes the red cotton reels so much. Why, you're a big girl now, Kathie."

Oh yes, the letter, the letter Kathie wrote, she did get it, but they don't have a job here, she's afraid. Times are so bad, you have to think whether you can hire any help at all. But she's been asking around, and the lawyer whose lady wife is such a good customer of theirs, that family is looking for a maid, a kitchen maid, and it would be a good place for Kathie.

Kathie lets Frau Hofmann write down the address on a piece of paper, and promises to go and introduce herself to the lawyer and his lady wife right away. But even as she puts the scrap of paper in her pocket she knows she won't. She isn't planning to be a kitchen maid. She could have gone into service back home in Wolnzach. But she doesn't let Frau Hofmann know what she's thinking. She smiles and thanks her for her help, and says of course she'll go and see the lawyer.

And how are things at home in Wolnzach? Frau Hofmann asks. Her mother was still going around the villages with her wares, says Kathie, and her father, oh, well, he was getting grumpier and grumpier. He wanted her, Kathie, out of the house. That's why she's come to the big city, that's why she's here in Munich. She'd hoped it would be easier to find a place here than at home in the village.

She'd met such a very nice girl who came to the country for the hop-picking last autumn, she says, and now she was staying with her here in Munich. She has a lovely, bright apartment, says Kathie, and she, Kathie, likes it there a lot. She doesn't want to go back home anymore. Back to her strict father and her mother. She thanks Frau Hofmann again for being so helpful. Then Kathie goes away, with the piece of paper in her pocket.

She crumples it up before she's turned the next corner. It's a lovely sunny day in Munich. The air is still warm, almost like spring. She sits on a park bench in the English Garden, and the sun warms her. The crumpled scrap of paper is in her coat pocket. She sits there watching the people strolling past. It's not long before a couple of guys sit down on the bench beside her. She laughs and jokes with them. One of them tells her he has a motor-bike, he could take her out into the country on it if she likes. Kathie is enthusiastic, of course she'd like that. They decide to go on a date, he writes his name and address down on a piece of paper for her so that she won't forget him. And she doesn't put this note in her coat pocket with the other one. She puts it in her little black bag instead.

In the evening she goes to Soller's in the valley. The blond man is there again. So is Anna. She lets the blond man buy her a meal, and they go to one of the rooms for rent at Soller's to sleep.

Herta

Johann Würth, that's my name. I work driving a truck for the firm of Friedrich Fischer. It'll be about eight years I've been working for Fischer's. I collect the milk from the dairy farms.

Same route every day. Around three in the afternoon I drive away from the station where they load the milk. I drive out along Landsbergerstrasse to Pasing. Then it's on to Freiham, Germering, Gilching, Argelsried and so to Wessling. I stop for a break in Wessling. I've done half my round when I get to Wessling, and I stop to eat a snack there. My wife packs me up a sausage sandwich, and I have tea or coffee in my thermos flask too. And about eight I drive the same way back to Munich. But not until I've loaded up the milk.

Well, not exactly the same route every day, but almost. Because on the way back from Wessling by way of Gilching I use the state highway. The stretch from Wessling to Munich. By this time I've been to almost all the dairy farms, and on the way back I just have to stop in Germering. Then I turn off the state highway again at Unterpfaffenhofen, and from there I go along the old road to Germering. That's right on the road. I load up the milk there, and by the time I go on it's nine o'clock. I do that route every day, the same round, day after day.

And I see the woman on her bike almost every day on the road from Germering to Munich. Always at the same time. She's always going along that stretch of road. Same as me. You could set your watch by her. I've often wondered what she does.

For a job, I mean. Because she's always going the same way at the same time. She must be on her way home from work, I've said to myself. Because if she was on her way to visit someone she wouldn't always be going the same way at the same time. She'd be earlier sometimes and later other times, depending. I can tell it's the woman cyclist by her woolen jacket. She wears it every day. Well, sometimes she wears it, other days she's strapped it on the carrier of the bike behind her.

That girl is always on her own. Always cycling along the road from Pasing to Germering, never going the other way. I've never seen anyone with her either, and I see her almost every day. She cycles really fast. I've noticed that too. She steps on those pedals good and hard. She's a stylish cyclist, that girl. She knows what she's doing, she's a good strong cyclist, I've told myself.

I'd have put her age at about 20, 25 at the most. That's why I call her a girl. Can't describe her any closer than that, though. I've only seen her late in the evening, and only from behind. But I've recognized her right away by her cardigan.

It's some dark color, I think either black or blue. Yes, I guess it would be dark blue. A dark blue woolen cardigan. The traditional kind.

On the Tuesday, well, I was going the same way as usual and I saw the girl again.

It was on the same stretch of road. Just after Germering and just before the road joins the state highway. I knew her at once. From her cardigan. This time it was on her carrier.

I couldn't see her face. Although I tried. She put her hand up to the side of her face in case the headlights dazzled her. Though I'd dimmed them on purpose, but the headlights on my truck are strong. I was thinking: there she is again. Always the same time of day. You really could set your watch by her.

And she was cycling on her own too.

Then I passed her quite fast.

About 100 yards in front of the girl on the bike, so that'd be a little closer to Germering, I did see someone else that day. On the left-hand side of the road, looking at it from the way I was going, there was a man standing behind a tree in the wood. His bike was lying in the ditch. I could see it lying there clearly in my headlights. I sit quite high up in my seat, so you have a good view. And the headlights show everything good and clear.

When the beam of my headlights caught the man I'd have been about ten yards away from him. All of a sudden he moved away from the tree, the way I was coming from. As if he was looking out for someone. Looking exactly the way the girl on the bike was coming.

I said to myself: seems like he's on the look-out for someone. At least, that's the way it looked to me. Or as if he was watching someone but didn't want to be spotted himself.

I wondered if he was waiting for the girl.

I passed him too fast to be able to describe him more closely. He wore a flat cap, I'm sure of that, though. Can't say what else he was wearing. I drove past him at quite high speed. If I was to say how tall he was, well, I'd be guessing at that too. He was standing a little way back behind that tree, easy to get it wrong. And when he peered out like that from behind the tree he was bending his knees too.

Soon after that I turned on to the state highway, and by the time I was on Landsbergerstrasse I'd forgotten the whole thing, it's only just come back to my mind now you ask me about it.

*

This Tuesday evening had been a quiet one for Amalia Ferch, waitress at the Lochhausen station restaurant. It was usually quiet on Tuesdays, as she will tell the police officer later. People have to be at work next day, so there's only the regulars in the restaurant. They were sitting at their usual table, same as always. Mostly the better-off locals. They'd been playing cards, the game of "Sheep's Head," as they almost always did too. The fifty-pfennig, ten-pfennig and five-pfennig coins, no single pfennig pieces, were lying in the little saucers beside the beer-mats. They met for an evening drink most evenings, argued about politics, the Party, God knows what else. Or else they just met to play "Sheep's Head" and the other Bavarian card game called "Watten."

It was different on a Friday evening, the company was usually more mixed then. The workers had been paid their wages and were mingling with the other guests and the card-players. Usually at separate tables, and the stakes were a little lower too. During the week many of them couldn't afford more than a tankard of beer from the off-license stall. They'd send their children for it. "And make sure you get good measure. Dad's tired from his work today."

At weekends the customers changed again. That was when the people on outings from nearby Munich came. Many on bicycles, others by train. Sometimes, not often, fine folk with their own motor cars. Those townies came in for a bite to eat. Saturdays and Sundays were the busiest times. "We have the tables in the garden open then, and there's homemade cake and coffee in the afternoons. And that's when the guests like to order an eggnog or a nice sweet Mosel."

In the summer months some of the vacationers from Cologne, Berlin or other cities come here too. They arrive by train, stay a few days for the fresh summer air. Visit Munich, the "capital of the Movement," and some come especially for the Oktoberfest.

That day, it was the last day of August, was even quieter than usual. Amalia Ferch didn't mind that, it meant she could at least get home in good time. She always worked at the restaurant on Tuesdays and sometimes at weekends.

She was just wiping down the tables and tidying up the main room. The last card-players had left about ten minutes before when that man came into the restaurant at about three-quarters to twelve.

Amalia asked if he'd like half a liter of beer. He just nodded. She poured him his half and took it to his table.

She sat down herself at the side table next to the stove. He'd be going to catch the last train to Munich, that meant she'd have to wait another half hour until the train left. Not a very attractive prospect. She was tired this evening, she wanted to go home. Her legs ached after her long day's work, and she had quite a way to go on her bicycle before she got home and could lie down in bed at last.

She began leafing through the newspaper that was lying on the table by the stove. She could see the guest out of the corner of her eye. As he was about to drink from his glass for the first time he rose to his feet, put the glass to his mouth and drank standing.

Then he put his glass back on the table. Sat down on his chair again. But he didn't stay sitting for more than a moment. He reached for his glass again, stood up once more. Drank. However, this time he stayed on his feet after he had finished drinking and put the glass down on the table.

He shifted from foot to foot. Again and again. Almost running on the spot. Then he shook one leg. Amalia got the impression that the man was vibrating all over. His restlessness seemed almost tangible. She couldn't help looking at him all the time. Holding the newspaper, she stared over the top of it in the guest's direction. He didn't notice; he was standing sideways on to her. Looking straight ahead. She peered over her paper and could see his profile. His strong nose, his chin. Smooth-shaven cheeks. She could see a scab on his cheek. A scratch while shaving, she supposed. His forehead was covered by a flat cap pulled well down.

It was also unusual for a man to be wearing an overcoat on such a mild day. A coat of some brownish color. She thought the fabric was loden, it had no belt, it was just a loose coat smooth at the back. With long pants, also brownish. He must have been about thirty years old. Medium height, slim build as far as she could see.

She felt almost awkward about staring at him like that, but she couldn't account for his nervousness. The guest sat down once more and seemed a little calmer. Amalia turned back to the report she was reading in the newspaper.

Suddenly he jumped up again and hurried out of the restaurant without a word.

Thinking he was trying to leave without paying for his beer, Amalia dropped the newspaper and prepared to run after the stranger. But as she hurried by she cast a glance at the table with the half-empty glass on it, and saw the money he had left beside the glass.

Two ten-pfennig pieces, one fifty, and two single pfennigs.

She picked it up, relieved, and put it in her purse. Then she cleared away the glass, put the chairs up on the tables, seats downward, switched off the light, locked up and went home.

She didn't give the guest in the restaurant and his strange behavior another thought.

The incident came back to her mind only a few days later, when she heard about the girl.

*

As Lina Führer said in her statement to the police on September 1, 1937, it was about ten in the evening when she heard the screams.

That had been the previous evening, August 31, 1937, at about eleven o'clock. Frau Führer had gone up to the first floor of the presbytery. She was going to close the windows, the windows facing Germering. It had been a mild summer evening, so she changed her mind and didn't close the windows at once. She had leaned on the window sill, looking out into the night.

From that window you could see the state highway, as she told the police officer. She must have watched about twenty cars pass by as she looked out of the window. No, she hadn't been counting them, but she thought there'd have been about twenty.

She didn't stay there by the window long, only for about five minutes, maybe a little longer. She was sure of that. Then, just as she was about to close the windows, she heard that screaming.

Loud screaming and moaning, a woman's voice. And directly afterward the voice began saying the Lord's Prayer.

She was sure about the Lord's Prayer. She could hear the opening words of the prayer clearly and distinctly. "Our Father, which art in heaven . . ." The voice had been loud. And the prayer was the reason why she stood there and listened to it in the night.

But after the opening she heard only fragments of the prayer. "Hallowed . . . Thy name . . . ," and the voice sank lower and lower. "In Heaven . . . earth." It was almost drowned out by the sound of the trucks driving along the state highway, ". . . Thy will be done. . . ." Until she lost it entirely.

She went on standing there at the window for a while. She strained her ears, but she heard no more. Only the traffic on the road nearby, that was all. Then she closed the windows and went down to the ground floor. She kept thinking about the screaming and moaning, she couldn't explain them to herself.

But then she forgot them as she made preparations for what she had to do in the kitchen next day. When she finally went to bed 45 minutes later, she had put it all out of her mind.

Next morning, even before early Mass, she heard about the murder. It was Herr Mesner told her, or had it been the women in the Reverend Father's congregation? She wasn't sure, because the whole village was in great excitement. And then she remembered hearing that screaming and moaning, and the Lord's Prayer.

So she went to the Reverend Father and told him about it, and he thought she ought to go straight to the police and inform them. She was rather reluctant, didn't want to get mixed up in anything. But the Reverend Father said it was her duty to go to the police and tell them what she had heard. She was an honest Christian woman, he said, and she might be able to help that poor girl's soul if she assisted the police in their attempts to find the guilty man.

So that was why she was here now in the police station, making a statement about what she had heard.

(Interrogation of Josef Kalteis, continued)

—Of course I heard about Herta's murder, and I knew her too.
—I was in the same gym as her brother, Franz is his name.
—The Eichenau Gym.
—I'm not so active there now. But I still go to the regulars' table at the inn. Always on Fridays.

—I saw Herta now and then too. A striking brunette, she was. You could really like her.

—Everyone knew about the murder, what happened to her, it went around the district like wildfire.

—A fellow that'll do a thing like that deserves hanging. I'd hang him upside down by his balls and cut his prick off. Chop!

—I'd make short work of him!

—A terrible thing, it was. I heard it was just before her wedding. Folks say she was going out with an SA man.

Tuesday and Wednesday

Tuesday passes much like Monday. Kathie wanders around the city during the day. For a moment she toys with the thought of looking for a job as a maid after all. Had she been too quick to crumple up the piece of paper with the address in her coat pocket? Should she go to the employment office and ask them where she can find a place? But then she doesn't after all. What else could she do, go to the hotels and boarding houses, ask if they need a chambermaid or a general servant? No she doesn't want to work as a maid. She'll be sure to find something else. She'll find something better than working as a servant for other people, kowtowing to them all the time. She only has to look at Mitzi, she's done it, and she, Kathie, would manage too. Mitzi lives very comfortably on the money she gets from her fiancé, the man in Gelsenkirchen. Why shouldn't she try the same thing? Hadn't Hans said what a nice clean girl she is? The city itself entices her, the sweet life of the city. Walking around, going for a stroll, looking at all the people. She'll make it, she's sure of that. And hasn't she managed very well so far? She's wanted for nothing yet, even without working she's had enough to eat and a place to sleep. She's young, her life lies ahead of her.

She strolls through the city. She buys herself a patent leather belt in a shop in the city center. It's black. She puts it on at once. She's seen other girls wearing belts like this, city girls. It's modern. She puts her old belt away in her handbag. The new one looks much better. The blond man had given Kathie the money for the belt. Not that she'd asked him for anything, she wouldn't do that, but he just gave her the money in the morning, telling her to buy herself something pretty. It wasn't much, but enough for the black belt and something to eat, and Kathie was happy with that.

In the evening she goes back to Soller's. By now she knows almost everyone there. The local peddler, Limping Anton, who goes his rounds at Soller's every evening with his vendor's tray slung around him, is making eyes at her again. "So here's our pretty Kathie back. Don't you think we'd make a good couple?" he calls out as she comes in through the door, winking his one eye and pursing his lips into a kissing shape.

Kathie laughs at him. "Oh, go along with you! You're far too old for me," she tells him. She felt like saying: you limp, and you have a glass eye, and you're a pauper, going around with your tray of shoelaces. But then she didn't like to.

Mitzi is there with dark-haired Hans, and she joins them. Anna only stays for a little while this evening. But it's still fun even without Anna, with just Hans and Mitzi. And it's Hans who suggests that Kathie could go and sleep at Mitzi's place tonight, since the blond man hasn't turned up and Kathie has nowhere else to go. She's happy with the idea, she doesn't have to think twice about it, so she goes to Mariahilfplatz with the two of them. They leave Soller's before closing time.

As they unlock the apartment, there's Anna already lying on the sofa in the kitchen living room. Anna is fast asleep, however hard Kathie shakes her she just keeps on sleeping. So she simply goes into the bedroom with the others. **She sleeps on the join where the twin beds are** pushed together, in between dark-haired Hans and Mitzi.

In the middle of the night Hans puts his hand out to Kathie, and she doesn't push it away. She says nothing, doesn't move, just lies there. Keeps still. He caresses her body with his hand.

*

The way Kathie lies so still is to strike the chauffeur too, later. The chauffeur she meets at Soller's on Wednesday evening.

He's sitting at the next table, and keeps looking across at the girl sitting between dark-haired Hans and Mitzi. There's a blond man at the table with them too. His back is turned to the chauffeur.

The girl keeps looking at him as well, and he smiles back. Raises his glass to her. Never takes his eyes off her. She has long, dark hair, woven into a braid. A round girlish face with rosy cheeks and round dark eyes. A big mouth with firm, full lips. He liked the look of her at once when he saw her sitting at the next table.

Sometime during the evening she stands up and goes toward the door. Just before she gets there she turns to him. He thinks she is smiling at him, just him. With her full lips and her brown eyes. Gives him a sign, a little nod, barely visible. She wants him to follow her.

He drinks some more of his beer and then goes out. She is waiting for him there. He feels uncertain, hardly knows what to say to her. Finally he asks if that fellow at her table, the one with the fair hair, is her boyfriend?

"No, just someone I know. He comes in here at Soller's quite a bit."

"Then you could move over to my table, what do you think?"

"No, you move over to us."

"But will that be all right with the others at your table?"

"It'll be fine with Hans. I'd have moved to your table before, but Hans thought I ought to wait. And he said if you liked me you'd move to our table. Otherwise it wouldn't do." As she speaks she plays with the braid hanging over her shoulder. Keeps passing it through her fingers. Her eyes are on him all the time. Smiling at him.

"I'm going back inside now. You wait here a moment and then come in too."

He does as she says. Stays in the middle of the path up to the inn. Waits, counts up to sixty the way kids do when they're playing hide and seek, and only then does he go back to where he was sitting. He finishes his beer and looks across at the girl as he drinks it.

Putting his hand in his pocket, he takes out the money for his drink, counts it, and puts it down beside the glass. Only then does he go over to the next table.

May he join them? His voice sounds to him strange and wooden. And the dark-haired man says, "Yes, of course, just sit down. So long as you're not the sort to **put on airs** you're welcome. All alone at your table, eh?"

He even gives up his place beside the girl so that the chauffeur can sit down beside her. And then they talk to each other all evening.

She tells him she's from Wolnzach. Her father deals in hops, her mother runs a general store. She's looking for a job here in Munich. Wolnzach was too countrified for her. She'd been working in a hotel there, that was her last job, she'd like one the same in Munich. She was really supposed to be staying with family, that had all been agreed, but they didn't have room for her, so she's putting up at Hans and Mitzi's place. They live in Mariahilfplatz.

He keeps looking at her as she tells him all this. He looks into her big dark eyes, he looks at her full lips. She has pretty teeth. Her voice is soft and gentle.

She goes on talking and talking. About her home in Wolnzach, how her father didn't want her living there anymore, so that's why she was here to look for a job.

Only much later does he ask what her name is. Katharina, she says. Katharina Hertl. But he can call her Kathie, everyone does.

They all stay late this evening, they don't leave until nearly midnight. The chauffeur asks Kathie if he can come back to Mariahilferplatz with her.

"Yes, I don't mind."

The night outside is starry, you can smell autumn already, taste it in the cold air. They cross the Viktualienmarkt, the big Munich produce market, passing the stalls closed down for the night. Mitzi and Hans are ahead of them.

First the chauffeur just walks along beside Kathie, then in Reichenbachstrasse he takes her arm, she feels a little cold, and they cross the Reichenbach Bridge arm in arm. When they reach the lodging-houses in Ohlmüllerstrasse, Hans turns to the pair of them. He calls back, over his shoulder, "Come on, time you two said goodnight."

Kathie stops. She goes quite close to the chauffeur. She whispers in his ear: will he be coming back to Soller's again tomorrow? He feels her breath on his skin, her warm breath.

"At nine," he hears her saying.

And when he nods Kathie kisses the chauffeur goodbye. He feels her lips on his. They are soft, warm and full.

Erna

I work for BMW in Munich. **Running in the cars.** My name is Georg Spielberger. I'm Erna's fiancé.

Erna and me, we met in February at the Salvatorkeller ball. It was February 3, 1934, Carnival Saturday.

I'd be lying if I said I didn't like her right away. The moment I first set eyes on her. I'd gone along with my friend Arthur Vogel and a few other guys. We were all dressed up as chimney sweeps. "Then the girls will kiss us for good luck and all that." It was Arthur's idea, he's always getting brainwaves like that. Erna was there with her girlfriend.

She came up to our table because she knew Arthur. She'd met him through her brother. I liked the look of her at once. She was dressed in a Pierrot costume, with a little cap on her head and a red heart painted on her cheek.

The two girls sat down at our table. I made sure she was sitting next to me, didn't want to give the other guys a chance. I never took my eyes off her all evening, and I didn't dance with anyone else.

When she told me she was in the office at the BMW Works, I said to her, "What a coincidence! I work at BMW too."

"You must be joking! I don't believe it," she said.

Arthur, who was standing behind me, had to back me up or she'd never have believed it.

She added, "How funny we've never met in the canteen or around the place somewhere else."

"It's certainly funny, because I'd have noticed you right away," I answered her back. "A pretty girl like you would catch anyone's eye."

She laughed heartily. She laughs a lot anyway, she likes laughing. She's a girl who enjoys life. That's why I liked her so much from the start. She's pretty too. That long, dark hair. Those black eyes. She really does have black eyes, and when she laughs they begin to sparkle. And she has a perky, heart-shaped little mouth. When she laughs you can see all her teeth.

I took her to her trolley stop, it was Line 1 on the Landsberger Bridge. And before she got on the trolley I plucked up all my courage and gave her a hug and a kiss. I thought to myself, this is the girl I've been looking for and I'm never going to let her go.

The very next day we met again, and then it was every day after that. We meet at work anyway, and I always wait for her outside the BMW gate after work.

The girls that Erna works with up in the bookkeeping department all know me. And if she's rather late coming out, I go up to her office and wait there.

Then after work we go to the movies, or for a walk, or just to my place. I'm still living with my parents, and when Erna realized that my mother always comes home from her job very late, she said, "I tell you what, I'll cook for you." And that's what we did. My Erna is a good cook.

She stays the night most weekends, and sometimes during the week too. Whenever we can't stop talking and telling each other stories and it's very late. Or when we've been to the movies.

She likes going to the movies, my Erna does, so we see almost all the new films they show at the movies. She can sing the songs from the films as soon as she's heard them. My Erna has a lovely voice. I always like listening to her. I've often said to her, "How can you remember that? You've only just heard it. I could never do it, honest."

Then she just laughs and shakes her head. "Oh, it's easy."

Quarrel? No, we never really quarrel. Now and then we exchange a few words, about some small thing, but no, we never have anything you might call a quarrel.

Last Saturday she came to my place around five-thirty. And around seven we went out. We went into town on the trolley.

Erna wanted to go to the Buttermelcherhof restaurant where her friend is a waitress. The friend's first name is Fanny. I'm afraid I don't know her surname or her address. Erna told me Fanny was at school with her, and they've been friends ever since. Every day in the morning Erna used to call for Fanny, she lived on her way to school. There were lots of other children in Fanny's family, Erna told me, and they had a billy-goat, one of her brothers was always setting it on the girls.

And we did have a word with Fanny in the restaurant, but then we decided to leave because it was very full. First we tried to find a place to sit, but we soon saw it was hopeless, so we left again after a few minutes.

I said to Erna why didn't we go to the movies, but she didn't want to, not that evening, so we went to the Wartburg in Auenstrasse to dance. Erna didn't dance with anyone but me all evening, she didn't dance with anyone else. We danced almost all the dances. I thought I'd never seen my Erna look lovelier than she did that evening. She was wearing her red dress with the white dots, and the yellow silk cord necklace with the little beads in it. I gave it to her for her birthday. On August 13, a day before the Ascension of the Virgin Mary. We got engaged that day, Erna and me.

We left the Wartburg bar around eleven-thirty. Then we walked almost as far as the Ludwig Bridge and sat down on a bench there.

I put my arm around her, and she leaned against me. We stayed sitting on that bench for quite a while. We still had plenty of time before the trolley left.

We agreed that next day, Sunday, she'd come to my place by two o'clock and we'd go out to Pasing, to see friends of ours. There's a fair in Pasing at the moment.

"Wouldn't you rather stay here, or why don't I take you all the way home?" I asked Erna, but she just laughed at me, she said I was fussing like a mother hen, and she could find her own way home even if she was blindfolded.

"It's all brightly lit," she said, "and it's not that far from my place. You know how fast I walk, it won't take me fifteen minutes."

"Yes, I know, but there's no one out and about at this time of night."

"There you are, then, there's nothing for me to worry about. And you'd have to go all the way back on foot, and then I'd be worrying about you."

She laughed when she said that. Suddenly I wasn't sure if she was laughing with me or at me. So I just kissed her.

Then we got up from the bench and went over to the trolley stop. We met Walter Schnabl there, he's an old school friend of mine. He was standing at the stop too, with his girlfriend. I think the girlfriend's name is Hilde, but I'm not sure. I only met her that one time. I was glad to think that they'd both be going at least a part of the way with Erna. Walter was taking his girlfriend home, and he said they'd be in the same trolley as Erna as far as Marienplatz. At Marienplatz Erna had to change to a number 6 trolley. I asked her again if she wouldn't like me to see

her home, but she just shook her head and laughed. Then the
trolley came along, and I saw all three of them getting in. Erna
found a window seat and waved. I waved back, I stood there
until the trolley had left. It wasn't until the trolley had turned
the corner that I turned and went home on foot.

*

Have you heard? About Fräulein Schmidlechner? They say
she's missing. Our Erna.

She's gone missing. She never came home on Saturday night.
Her parents are frantic. They've been searching everywhere.

It was in the city. She met her fiancé there and then she
never came home that evening.

Something must have happened to our Erna ... Because she
hasn't come home. That's not like her at all. She's very consci-
entious. She works in the bookkeeping department at BMW.
Just like her father and her brothers, they all work at BMW too.
Her fiancé as well. So I've heard.

At first her parents thought she'd stayed overnight in town
with her fiancé. Seems she often stayed the night there. In
the city.

So that's why they thought nothing of it at first when she
didn't come home. On Saturday night.

But when she didn't go to the office on Monday, and neither
her father nor her fiancé knew where she was, that's when they
went to the police.

They reported her missing, and since then everyone's been
looking for Erna.

They even want to search with dogs, because by now the
police are assuming it's a crime.

Seems there was a gentleman who asked her now and then
if she'd like a ride in his car. She told her mother about it,

that's what her auntie Frau Huber told me. Frau Huber from Rehstrasse, maybe you know her.

And I've heard it's an act of revenge.

There's a rumor it was her doing that some people from around here got sent to Dachau. Communists. She's said to have denounced them. But no one knows anything for sure.

I don't want to know all the details, you can easily get involved in something, and who knows, then you might end up in Dachau yourself. They'll have had skeletons in their cupboards for sure, those folk.

*

Theresa Pirzer heard it first from her mother, they say, when she came home from shopping. "Erna Schmidlechner has gone missing. She hasn't been home since Saturday. They're looking for her everywhere. The police are even searching with dogs." She couldn't believe it, she'd seen Erna on Saturday night. She went to Erna's' mother.

She wanted to know if the rumor was true, if Erna really hadn't gone home. It was only then that she went to the police.

Yes, that was right, she'd seen Erna on Saturday. She'd been in the same trolley, it was Line 6, she'd been on her way home around ten past one that night. Theresa Pirzer had been in the Winzerer Bierhalle dancing that Saturday evening, and got into the same trolley, that's when she saw Erna.

Except for her and her husband and Erna there was just one other passenger in the trolley to Milbertshofen, a man. She's certain of that, she says. But she didn't know who he was.

She sat down with Erna and had a word with her. Erna told them she'd been in town with her fiancé. They'd been out dancing, they had a really nice time.

At the terminus they all got off the trolley. The man went the other way, Theresa's sure of that too.

Right after they got out they said goodbye to Erna. Theresa and her husband got their bikes. They'd left them at the trolley station so they wouldn't have to walk home.

When they reached the old Milbertshofen cemetery they met Erna again. They cycled past her. Just as they were passing Erna, when they drew level with her, they saw a gentleman's bicycle leaning against a lamppost. Two men were standing a little way off. Theresa thought that was odd, so she turned and saw one of the two men speak to Erna. Theresa saw Erna turn her head to the men, but she went on without thinking any more of them.

The men would have been around thirty, so far as she could tell, but she can't be sure of that.

When she reached the South German Brakes works, right by the snack bar, she looked around for Erna Schmidlechner again.

She saw Erna going off by herself toward her parents' apartment. There was no sign of the two men anymore.

Soon afterward she met another family from the neighborhood, on the way home with their baby in a pram.

Today, after she talked to Erna's mother and before she went to the police station to make a statement, she looked in on that family specially. They too told her they'd seen a girl in a red dress. On her own, no one with her. It was a little way from the snack bar, they're sure of that. She asked about the men, but they didn't know anything about any men.

If anything's happened to Erna, it could only have happened around the landfill and gravel pit just behind South German Brakes, she's sure of that. Because the whole way is well lit with the street lamps, and she can't imagine that anyone, not those two men, would dare to attack someone in bright streetlighting.

*

There he suddenly is standing in front of her, that fellow. Confronting her, legs planted wide apart. His flat cap pulled down over his face—and that horrible grin. It was even broader than before. Just now, not five minutes ago, the guy had spoken to her. He was grinning then too. Standing beside the other man. There was no sign of the other man now. Only the one with the flat cap was there.

He'd called something out to her as she passed him. She hadn't really heard it. Didn't want to know what it was either. But she'd turned, and he was grinning in her face.

Bastard, she thought to herself. She'd heard a laugh behind her back, and she walked faster. No, she wasn't afraid. The street was brightly lit, and she wasn't alone. Theresa Pirzer and her husband on their bikes were still within earshot.

But all the same, she suddenly wished she had Georg with her. She shouldn't have told him not to come. But then he'd have had to go all the long way back. No, it would have been better to stay with him tonight. It would definitely have been better. She was sorry now she hadn't.

Even as she was thinking of Georg, the other man, who was wearing a peaked cap, cycled past her. And when she came to the South German Brakes factory, she met that couple with their baby. She asked why they were out so late with their child. He was sitting in his pram. His mother was pushing it and his father walking along beside her. It was just before reaching the snack bar she met them.

She knew that snack bar well. She'd been a trainee in the factory. She bought herself something at the snack bar almost every time they had a lunch break. The other girls used to laugh at her. She always bought the same thing. Every day. A doughnut. Then she took out the middle of it. She removed the inside, the jam and the doughy bit around it, and always put it aside. After that she filled the doughnut itself with smoked sausage.

How odd to think of that just now. They'd fired her after she finished her training, and she'd never bought a doughnut at that snack bar again. Now she buys her doughnuts in the works canteen. But she still hollows them out and fills them with smoked sausage. The girls in the bookkeeping department at BMW laugh at her and shake their heads, just the way they did at the South German Brakes factory.

With all this going through her head, she hardly noticed the fellow with the sporting cap. She never saw him leave his bike beside the snack bar and stand in her way.

Legs planted wide apart, and grinning.

"Well, got time for me now? I sent my friend home."

"Leave me alone."

"Now, now, not so much of your cheek! You come along and keep quiet, and then you won't be hurt. I need it now, here, come on, don't make such a fuss. You and your fat ass. Wow, I liked that the moment I saw it."

"Leave me alone, you bastard. Go away! I don't want anything to do with you!"

She tries to pass him.

When she's level with him, right beside him, he grabs her by the throat.

So fast, so suddenly—she hadn't been expecting it.

She defends herself. She's not putting up with this. She flails out. He's stronger. All the same, he has difficulty holding on to her. He pulls her down on the ground. "Stop that, you're making me even wilder for it Slut!"

She tries everything. Twists and turns. Hits out. Tries to scratch him, bite him. Fight back, fight back, fight back, that's all she can think.

"Bastard. Let me go!"

"Keep still or I'll finish you off! Keep still, will you?"

She won't keep still. She doesn't want to keep still. Feels something cold and metallic at the back of her neck. And then pain that almost makes her faint away.

She wants to go on fighting back. She wants to hit out. Not give in. In spite of the pain. She wants, she wants, she wants . . .

But neither her arms nor her legs will obey her anymore. She can't move, can't move at all. She can't move anymore! Panic takes her in its grip. What has that bastard done to her? What has he done?

She screams. And screams. Screaming is all that's left to her, the only thing she can do. She screams, lying there on the ground behind the kiosk. She's screaming for her life. Because of the pain. In spite of the pain. Screaming as long as she can. Screaming and screaming.

The cyclists, the family—the mother, father and child—someone must hear her. Oh, surely they must hear her.

The man won't let her go. She feels his body lying on hers.

Feels it heavy as a hundredweight. Can't push him away. Can't shake him off. Can't move. Can't move anymore.

Bastard, bastard, bastard!

He has something in his hand. A piece of fabric. She recognizes it.

It's the white fabric of her underwear.

That bastard has taken her underwear off.

He holds the fabric, he stuffs it far into her mouth with his hands.

She can't defend herself anymore. She just lies there, unable to fight back. He stuffs the underwear deep between her jaws. The screaming dies away.

She wants to retch. Feels the pain in her jaws. Realizes she can't breathe anymore. Desperately, she tries to get some air. Air, air! There's less and less of it. She is fighting desperately for air. Air!

She can't scream. Can't scream. Can't breathe. Nothing. No air. None.

THURSDAY AND FRIDAY

The chauffeur comes into Soller's at eight-thirty. Half an hour before they arranged to meet. He's eager to see the girl again. Hasn't been able to settle to anything all day. If he began work on something he stopped again and put it off until later. Just after six he sets off from home. He goes all the way to Soller's in the valley on foot. He doesn't take the trolley, doesn't want to be even earlier.

Once he's reached the inn he soon finds her. She's sitting at the same table again. They're all there, just like the day before, Hans sitting between Kathie and Mitzi. Even the blond man is in the same place, as if they had never left Soller's at all.

He's still in the doorway of the bar at Soller's when she sees him. She jumps up at once and goes over to him.

"Hello, why are you so early? I wasn't expecting you yet. Come and join us." She doesn't let him get a word in edgeways. She looks radiant, her eyes shining with delight. He feels her take his hand. Her hand is soft and warm in his. The chauffeur hesitates just for a moment, slightly withdraws his hand, but then he lets her lead him over to the others at the table. He sits down beside her.

Once again she talks to him all evening. The words spill out of her. She went to the Wiesn again today. Has he ever been out there himself? She rode on the roller-coaster. It was lovely, she screamed out loud because you get such a funny feeling inside you when the car goes rushing down. Such a tingling feeling, she can hardly describe it. And then she went on the swingboats too. "I swung and swung. I swung right up to the sky. A little higher, I thought, and I'll be flying into the clouds like a bird, I felt so light. Of course I know that wouldn't happen, but when you swing up so high you feel you don't weigh anything, you really think for a moment, just for the fraction of a second, just for the blink of an eyelid that you could fly. It makes you feel so good!"

She gets quite heated with all this talking. Her cheeks are red, and her eyes are shining more than ever. She'd been on the swingboats before, at a fair when she went on a pilgrimage with her godmother. As a little girl. She tells the chauffeur about it.

She and her mother had gone to see her godmother. She wasn't yet ten. And then they went on from where her god-mother lived to Eichelberg. "That's quite a long way. We started early in the morning while it was still dark. We walked to the church through the night, and when we got there it was still dark." They'd gone into the church with all the other pilgrims. Out of the dark night right into the church, which was brightly lit with candles. It looked as if heaven had opened. As if they were in Paradise itself, she tells him, it was all so bright. And then, after the church service, they went to the fair. She was allowed to ride the chairoplane and go on the swingboats. And then there were the stalls. She went from stall to stall with her auntie, she never tired of looking at them. She couldn't decide which had been the best part of that day, the candles in church or the fair.

While she talks and talks, the chauffeur keeps looking at the girl. He likes her more and more with every word she speaks. Her rounded face, her voice, he likes everything about her. He sits there looking at her. He sits there without a word, never taking his eyes off her. Just listening to the sound of her voice. So soft and warm. He looks into her face, into her eyes, would like to touch her, feel her warm body, wants to feel her very close to him. He is slightly afraid she might be able to read his thoughts in his eyes, and yet he wants that more than anything. Late in the evening they set out from the inn. It must be after midnight when Kathie goes home across the Viktualienmarkt with the chauffeur, as she did on Wednesday. They walk the same way as yesterday. Only this time he puts his arm around her waist right at the start. And they kiss for longer when they say goodnight. They agree to meet at midday tomorrow. On the Reichenbach Bridge, by the news stand. He sees her beside the news stand long before he gets there. Kathie in her green coat, unbuttoned, with her blue dress and the patent leather belt under it. Her blue hat on her head. It sits perkily on her head, more like a cap. A light breeze keeps blowing its pale ribbons into her face. She stands there by herself, waiting for him.

He stops, looks at her from a distance before she sees him, hesitates before going right up to her. Kathie puts her arms around him, holds him close and kisses him on the mouth. Soft, warm lips on his mouth.

"Come on, we're going out to my little property. I have a log cabin out in Waldperlach. Come with me," he tells her. Kathie looks at him and nods. He takes her hand in his. Hand in hand, they go to the trolley stop. They ride out to Giesing station, and then go on by train toward Neubiberg In the train she tells him she hadn't been waiting for him long. Only five minutes, no more. She didn't get up until eleven this morning. Not that she slept until then, but she got up late. She'd had such a good time with Hans and Mitzi. Hans had teased her, and she teased him back. He demanded a kiss as a forfeit, otherwise he said he'd pull the covers of the bed off her. Mitzi just stood there laughing.

They spend all afternoon in the log cabin, the chauffeur and Kathie. They sit on the veranda in the sun. He puts his arm around her and kisses her. She teases him, asks if he takes her for just another of those girls—the girls who'll always go up to the bedrooms at Soller's with the gentlemen. "Because I'm not like that."

No, he doesn't take her for one of those girls at all, what makes her think so? Although he doesn't understand why she isn't staying with her relatives. Her relatives in Munich that she told him about at the start. Wouldn't it have been easier for her to stay there, instead of with Mitzi and Hans?

She just looks into his eyes and doesn't answer. He strokes her face, tenderly kisses her mouth, her throat, the back of her neck.

"Well, I'm not one of that sort, don't you worry. I've never been up to one of the bedrooms at Soller's with anyone, I've never slept with anyone." She's still a virgin, she tells him as she walks to the log cabin with him. He doesn't believe a word of it, but that doesn't matter to him.

Neither of them has said a word. They are quite calm as they undress inside the log cabin. He hangs his jacket over the back of the chair, takes off the rest of his clothes, folds them carefully and puts them down beside the jacket. She undresses too, slips quickly into the bed standing in the corner of the room. She feels the smooth, starched linen on her bare skin. Waits there, ready for him, as he lies down in the bed beside her. He lies very close. She feels his breath on her skin. Feels his hands on her body. The little light falling in through the small window of the room gives her skin a pale glow. He strokes her face with his hand, he caresses her body. Takes a deep breath. Closes his eyes, concentrates entirely on what he feels, what he smells. On her body, on the smell of her.

She lies there perfectly still.

Lies still as he strokes her breasts, her back, her legs.

Lies still as he kisses her. On the mouth, on the throat, on the breasts. The firm white breasts of a young girl.

Lies still as he rolls on top of her, feeling her warm body under him.

Lies still as he caresses her down there with his hand, as he kisses her.

Lies still as he touches her with his fingers, gently spreads her legs with his hand.

Lies still as he comes inside her. Feeling every part of her warm, moist body now.

She keeps still the whole time.

It is this stillness that will linger in his memory later.

After he has made love to her he gets off the bed. Gets dressed the way he undressed, without a word. His pants, his shirt, his socks, his shoes.

Goes out into the garden. Goes out without turning to look at her, out to do some work there.

She, Kathie, stays lying in the bed.

Only later does he come back into the log cabin, where she is sitting on the chair at the kitchen table. She has put her blue dress on again, and the black patent leather belt over it. He notices how high she wears the belt, almost below her breasts. His wallet is lying on the table in front of her. She has taken it out of his jacket pocket without asking him. She is holding the photographs he carries around in his wallet, just sitting there looking at the pictures. Letting photo after photo slip through her hands. As he sees her sitting there holding his photographs displeasure rises in him, anger. He doesn't want this. He doesn't want her looking at his pictures. Doesn't want to let her into his life. He goes over to her, takes the pictures from her hand. It's a rough gesture, he almost snatches them away from her. He feels uncertain, he doesn't feel good. Aren't they his pictures, isn't it his life? She has no place in it. He doesn't want that, he never will.

He quickly puts the photos back in his wallet. Hears her asking if she can have one of them to keep, as a memento. He doesn't know if he says no or just shakes his head, but he hastily puts the pictures back where they belong, in his wallet, and puts the wallet back in his jacket.

But Kathie has kept one of the pictures after all, the one with the church of St. Corbinian in the background. She let it fall into her lap, and then slipped it into her handbag. He never noticed.

At six they catch the train back to Munich. She talks to him, acts as if the incident with the photos had never happened. He tries to ignore it too. So they sit there in the train, each of them trying to get across the wall that's suddenly risen between them by talking. The pauses in their conversation get longer. Sometimes they sit there without saying a word. They simply sit there.

They go back from Giesing Station by trolley to the Church of the Holy Ghost, where they say goodbye. The chauffeur gives her a quick kiss on the cheek. She doesn't want to let him go, asks if he won't come back to Soller's with her. It's still early in the evening.

No, not today, tomorrow, yes, they'd meet again tomorrow. He'd come to Soller's then. She must wait for him there. Does she like going to the movies? Well then, they could go to the movies. Has she seen that film, one of the new talkies? What was the title again? "In A Little Cake-Shop," she says at once, Mitzi kept singing that song. Yes, they could go and see that film.

"Won't you change your mind and come to Soller's with me? We could have something to eat there. I haven't eaten yet today," she says to the chauffeur again. "Not today, I'm afraid," he says, but he presses a mark into her hand to pay for a meal as he says goodbye. She watches him go, sees him walk down the street in his sports pants to just above the ankle with his flat cap on his head. She turns twice to look at him again. Waves to him before she goes on in the direction of Soller's in the valley. He has turned to look back at her as well, stands there, waiting until she is out of sight. Only then does he go on. He goes from the Church of the Holy Ghost into Theatinerstrasse. There he stops outside a shop and waits. Until a young woman comes out of the shop. His wife. He hugs her and asks what kind of a day she's had a work. She takes his arm, and they go back to the apartment they share arm in arm.

Marlis

Marlis Gürster, née Neumüller, reported missing on May 30, 1934. The young woman, age 26, left her husband's hairdressing salon around ten that Wednesday morning to go for a bicycle ride to Starnberg. She was last seen by passersby riding her bicycle in the Starnberg direction.

The missing woman is described as follows: about 5 feet 4 inches tall, round face, high forehead, small mouth, all her own teeth, stocky figure, black hair, bobbed hairstyle. She was wearing a blue and white dirndl dress at the time of her disappearance, white socks and white shoes. It is not known whether the missing woman had a coat or a jacket with her.

She was riding a Viktoria lady's bicycle.

She also had a black and white striped beachrobe with her, a red bathing suit and a small bag with her needlework in it.

According to a statement made by her husband, the missing woman planned to be back in her parents' apartment by seven in the evening at the latest. But when he did not find her there, and she did not come home all evening, he reported her missing.

Distinguishing marks: none. The missing woman
was wearing a wedding ring with the date 7.5.34
inside it, a gold bracelet and a gold-colored
lady's wristwatch.

Please report any useful information to Munich
Police, Missing Persons Department, telephone 4321,
extension 316.

*

I last saw my wife Marlis on May 30, 1934. She came to the
hairdressing salon around ten that morning. My salon is at
Number 11 Schleissheimerstrasse, Munich. Her parents' apartment is quite close, only a few streets away. We don't have an
apartment of our own yet, so we're living at her parents' place
for now, in her old room. Only for the time being, because we're
going to move into our own first apartment on July 1. My wife
and I are really looking forward to it—I'd say she looks forward
to it even more than me. I don't mind living with my parents-in-
law, I've always got along very well with them, especially my
mother-in-law. But then I'll admit I'm out at the salon most of
the day. When I get home we eat with my in-laws, and sometimes we all listen to the radio after supper, but not very often,
and then I go to our room. Marlis has been at home all day
since we married. The situation was a bit more difficult for her.
She wanted to get away from home, have our own apartment.
"Old and young don't belong under the same roof," that's what
my grandmother always said. Marlis quarrels with her parents
quite often, usually over little things. And more with her father
than her mother. "He still treats me like a child," she's said
to me.

Marlis can be very stubborn sometimes. When she thinks
she's right she doesn't mince her words, that's why there are

arguments between father and daughter. My wife's inherited her obstinacy from her father. I think it has to do with his job. My father-in-law was a police detective superintendent until he retired. I get along well with him because I like peace and quiet, so I just take care not to annoy him. But I think I have an easier time with him than Marlis, I'm only his son-in-law.

On Wednesday Marlis arrived in the salon around ten. Since giving up work herself she often visits me there in the morning. She used to be an office assistant in Dr. Semmelmann's law firm until we married. She liked working in the office there, but she gave up her job a few weeks ago. We're planning to run the Schleissheimerstrasse salon together. A hairdressing salon of my own, that's always been my dream, and Marlis thinks the same. We only recently took the business over, and in a few weeks' time, after we've moved house, my wife is going to come and work with me there. That's why she left her office job.

When she arrived at the salon on Wednesday she was a little annoyed. She'd been arguing with her father again. She told me it's been about which of them hadn't switched off the cellar light. One of those little things that they quarrel over. Marlis often forgets to switch off the light in the cellar when she goes down there to get something, and they usually quarrel over that. I must admit I wasn't really listening to her. My thoughts were elsewhere, and to be honest I get tired of all those arguments. It's childish if you ask me, like two little kids fighting over a toy in the sandbox. But my wife sometimes takes these quarrels very much to heart. I advised her not to get into them in the first place, but as I said, she has a mind of her own.

This little bit of trouble was the reason why Marlis planned to cycle to Starnberg that morning, too. "I feel so annoyed, I want to be out of doors for a while!" she told me. I didn't particularly like to think of her cycling to Starnberg on her own. I'd have preferred her to stay in the city. I tried to get her to change her mind. We could go out there on Saturday afternoon, I said, or Sunday when we have the whole day to ourselves. Just the two of us, and wouldn't it be nicer to go to Starnberg together? But my wife has her own ideas, and I couldn't persuade her otherwise.

"I can look after myself, silly, I'm a grown woman. Don't you get like my father—I'm warning you!" she said, laughing, and she kissed me on the forehead. In the doorway she turned again and said, "Oh, I'll be so glad when we're in our own apartment at last." She was going to meet me at the salon about seven. "And if the weather is still as fine as this we could go to a beergarden this evening, what do you think?" I went out of the door with her, she gave me another goodbye kiss, got on her bicycle and rode away.

So seven o'clock came, and I waited, but she didn't come. I stayed in the salon twenty minutes longer than usual on purpose. I mean, we'd agreed that she'd come there to meet me. So then, about twenty to eight, I was back at her parents' apartment. I'd hoped she'd be there and had simply decided not to come to the salon. But she wasn't. When she still wasn't home by ten, we didn't know what to do. My in-laws and I were very worried. We were afraid something might have happened to her. I went to the police station with my father-in-law to report her missing. My mother-in-law stayed at home, hoping Marlis would come back after all.

Try as I may, I can't think where she is. Something must have happened to her. The police officer on duty asked me if my wife might perhaps have harmed herself. I can't imagine that. Yes, she took those quarrels to heart, but not all that much. My wife is a lively, happy, intelligent woman. She has a great many interests. She paints, and she likes sporting activities. Only last Pentecost Sunday we went mountain-walking in Lenggries. My wife loves the mountains. It was a wonderful weekend. We spent the night on the Kotalm in the mountain hut on the pastures there. It was one of our best mountain-walking expeditions ever.

Suicide, no, I'm sure it can't be suicide. It simply wouldn't be like her. Not in her nature. And what reason could she have had? None! Our marriage is very happy and harmonious. She grew up in comfortable circumstances. She never had to spend a penny of her own salary. She was my in-laws' only child, and they were both getting a bit old when she was born, they'd almost given up hope of a baby when she came along. So her parents looked after her very well, even spoiled her. She had a very happy, carefree childhood and youth. No, I don't think she's harmed herself in any way.

And our relationship has always been very harmonious. We've been very happy together ever since I met her a year and a half ago in the Pinakothek art gallery in Barer Strasse. We were both looking at the collection of paintings, that's where I first saw her. I ran straight into her arms, literally. I wasn't looking where I was going and almost knocked her down. I felt very embarrassed, and she laughed. Then I knew she was the girl for me. You don't find a girl like that twice. I'd fallen in love at first sight. And then we married on May 7th.

Someone who enjoys life so much can't kill herself, she couldn't do anything to herself. She really has no reason. None at all. We were full of plans for the future: the salon, our apartment, we'd travel. We were planning to go to Italy. She's always wanted to see Italy, and next winter we were going to ski there and stay in a mountain hut, with friends. It's all planned.

We've looked for her everywhere. I was so desperate, I even let my mother-in-law persuade me to go and see a clairvoyant with her. Marlis would laugh at me if she knew. But what am I to do? I clutch at every straw in sight. I'd never have thought I'd do a thing like consulting a clairvoyant. But a good friend of my mother-in-law set it up, and my mother-in-law and I both went for the consultation. I was supposed to take along some personal item belonging to my wife, so I took her favorite dress. She wore it for our engagement party. The medium put the dress on a small round table in a darkened room, wrote the date of my wife's birth on a piece of paper and put the note on the dress. She had a little pendulum on a chain, and she began letting it swing over the objects. I felt like something out of the film *Dr. Mabuse*. I saw that film with my wife, and I knew how funny she would find all this. At that moment I knew the whole thing was useless. Just nonsense. And for the first time I felt I'd never see Marlis again, I knew she was never coming back. I wanted to leave, but I couldn't do that to my mother-in-law, couldn't leave her alone with that woman. That's the only reason I stayed. My mother-in-law was hoping for so much from this consultation. I couldn't disappoint her.

The clairvoyant said my wife had emigrated to South America and was living in a big white house there. But she feared for her life, because there was a dentist who meant her harm. You can see for yourself what nonsense the whole thing was. But I was so desperate, I was even prepared to let myself in for this baloney. Now I don't know what to do. A human being can't simply vanish, can she, dissolving into thin air?

*

He had to go out. He couldn't stand it at home anymore. Aimlessly, he rode around the area. As always when he was cycling.

How long had he been on the road? Hours, maybe. He had no idea. He was searching. He was restless.

She came cycling toward him. Blue and white dirndl dress. White socks and shoes. If he leaned a little way forward over his handlebars he could see under her skirt. It had slipped a little way up as the pedals went up and down. She had firm, sturdy legs. He loved legs like those. In his mind he passed his hand over them. His eyes went on. Up her legs. Her thighs were rubbing together. He saw the soft, warm skin of them, damp with sweat. If he concentrated very hard, he thought he could even see her underwear, her panties. White. White silk. Girls like this one wore white silk underclothes. Not that cheap, dingy cotton jersey stuff. Silk underwear, the kind you could buy in the expensive lingerie shops. What would those underclothes feel like on the skin? Cool. Cool on the skin, smooth between the fingers. He realized that his thoughts were exciting him. The sight of those legs moving up and down, her thighs rubbing together. He imagined what it would be like to part them. Thrust against her resistance. He wanted to feel her resisting him. Wanted to feel her twisting and turning under him.

He slowed down. Didn't want to pass her too soon. Wanted to enjoy the sight up till the last moment. Thought of the silk underclothes and the thighs rubbing together. And how he would push in between them.

He hoped she'd fight back. Brace herself against him with all her might. He wanted to smell her fear, taste her sweat. Heighten his excitement that way. He wanted to enjoy the moment, increase his pleasure.

He rode past her. She'd given him only a fleeting glance. Hadn't really seen him. Had hardly noticed him.

He'd give her a little time. Lull her into a sense of security. He rode on a little way in the opposite direction from her, then turned and started cycling after her. Pursuing her. Like a huntsman on the track of his prey. Didn't take his eyes off her. Once he was level with her again his chance had come. He grabbed her from the side. Pushed her off her bicycle. She was too surprised to defend herself, to make a sound, to scream. Next moment she was in control of herself again. She began fighting back. Kicked out at him with her legs.

He had dropped full length on her, his weight pressing her down. He felt the body under him, her writhing body. He held her by the throat. He squeezed it, not too firmly, but firmly enough. Wanted to keep her from screaming. Wanted to see fear take hold of her, wanted to see her defend herself. He wanted her to fight back, he wanted her to try to get free, that was part of the game. His game. He wanted to enjoy the moment. He couldn't enjoy it unless she fought back. One hand at her throat, he reached down to her legs with the other. Grasped at her crotch. Got hold of her vulva. Tried to pull her underwear down, roughly. Pressed a leg between hers and so forced them apart.

She never stopped fighting. That was good, he liked that. It excited him to feel her body under his, writhing like that, trying to turn away and shake him off. Oh, that was good, it was how he liked it.

"Carry on like that, would you, slut? Give up and keep still or I'll shoot you!" he hissed in her ear. She didn't keep still, she almost managed to escape. He pressed his thigh even harder between her legs, reached his free hand into his trouser pocket. Felt the cold metal of the revolver.

Took it out of his pocket. It felt good. Incredibly good. He held the gun to the back of her neck and pulled the trigger.

The shot rang out.

The body under him that had just been writhing went slack.

He felt her limbs relax. She had stopped moving. She was keeping still now.

He stood up. Took the girl by her legs and dragged her further into the undergrowth.

Even before he could touch her vulva he ejaculated.

He didn't leave the dead girl alone, even then. Thrust his knife into her, cut out her vulva. The body was his now, he could do whatever he liked with it. Once she was dead, she belonged entirely to him. She was his possession. He was still as aroused as ever, his excitement increased when he had her vulva in his hands, the piece of flesh he had cut out of her. He smelled it. He licked it, chewed at it, put the vulva over his own penis. That way he could imagine penetrating her at last. Thrusting right inside her. Finally he put the piece of flesh over her face. "There, lick yourself, eat yourself, slut!"

Only later, much later, did he dig a hole in the woodland floor with his little knife. How long it took him he can't remember. Only that it was almost dark by the time he had finished.

He tried to put the dead body in the grave.

Unsuccessfully. He hadn't dug it deep enough.

He cut into her flesh again with his knife. Cut deep, to the joint. Cut through the sinews, twisted the bone at the joint, freed it. Freed it from the hip joint. The crack of the bones and sinews intoxicated him all over again.

He put the dead girl's legs, now separated, on top of her torso and covered it all with earth, branches and leaves.

He removed all objects of any value she had on her. He found a few marks in her purse, and threw the empty purse heedlessly away. He took her bike on his shoulders. Wasn't going to leave it at the scene of the crime. He was afraid the dead girl might be found sooner if he did. Sitting on his own bike, carrying hers on his back, he set off. Hours had passed, darkness had fallen. He was cycling without any light, under cover of night, through villages whose names he didn't know. He cycled half the night until he thought he had put enough distance between himself and the dead girl. He stopped beside a canal. Put the girl's bicycle down. Tried to take it apart. He didn't want anyone feeling interested in a wrecked bike. He took his time. Removed the wheels from the bike, separated the tire and the inner tube. Cut both into small pieces with his knife. He dismantled even the spokes and the ball-bearings. He jumped on the framework of the bike as it lay on the ground with his whole weight. Once, twice. He can't say how often.

He felt as if the bicycle were resisting, the way its owner had fought back just now. That spurred him on, heightened his fury. When he left it, it would be no more use to anyone. No more use, like the body he had left on the woodland floor. He kept kicking it, stamping on the frame, jumping up and down on it. He picked it up and flung it to the ground. Picked it up again, flung it to the ground once more. He felt the sweat running down his body. He never stopped working the bike over. In the end he picked up what was left of it and threw it into the canal.

He looked at his dirty, bloodstained hands. Bent down, washed them in the cold water. Felt how much good the water did his hands. How much good it did him. He undressed, jumped into the canal, dived down under the water, black in the night. Felt how cool it was all around him. Felt himself slowly calming down in the dark water, felt how pleased he was with himself, how happy he was.

Back home, he took off his dirty, bloodstained clothes. Lay down naked in bed. Closed his eyes. Saw the girl before him once more. Realized that the idea of what he had done was exciting him all over again. He reached for his penis. Rubbed it while he thought of the girl, going through it all once again, step by step, enjoying it to the very end. Until, tired and exhausted, he fell into a deep sleep.

SATURDAY

Kathie is sitting in Soller's on Saturday. At the same table as usual. She can see the whole inn from there. She never takes her eyes off the door all evening. Every time it opens, her heart seems to stop for a brief moment. Every time she thinks now the chauffeur is coming through the doorway, and time after time she's a little more disappointed. She's been taking the photo out of her bag again and again that day. Holding it and looking at it again and again. As if the power of her gaze would be enough on its own to bring him here. She tenderly strokes his face with her fingers, the face in the photograph. The dark blond hair that he's combed back from his face and over to one side. She presses it close to her, caresses it.

The chauffeur is wearing an Alpine jacket in the photo. A dark Alpine jacket and sports pants ending just above the ankles. He stands in front of St. Corbinian's Church with his cap in one hand. She shows the picture to Mitzi, then to Anna. Holds it close again, kisses it once more. Countless times. Waits for him all day.

The chauffeur is waiting too. After all, he does want to see the girl again. He wants to touch her, kiss her, sleep with her.

Quite early, after breakfast, he went out with his wife to Waldperlach and his little property to spend all day there. Working in the garden, tidying up the beds ready for winter. The chauffeur keeps glancing surreptitiously at his watch. His wife notices his restlessness. What's wrong with him? she asks.

"Oh, nothing in particular. Why would there be anything wrong with me?" Only today, he says, he forgot all about meeting the regulars at his club, the soccer club. He has to get there, he tells her, he'd feel very bad about letting the regulars down today of all days. To his surprise his wife says she'll go with him, so they travel back from Waldperlach to Munich together.

Home in their apartment he snatches a moment to write to Kathie. A letter explaining why he can't meet her today as they agreed. Makes up a story to account for it. He tells her not to worry, he'll come to Soller's as soon as he can. Maybe tomorrow.

He puts the letter in his jacket pocket. He'll try to find a messenger boy to deliver it to Kathie.

The blond man has come to Soller's, not the chauffeur. He sits down at the table with Kathie. Asks if he can buy her something to eat. Kathie declines, hesitating. Because she still hopes the chauffeur will turn up. Finally she lets the blond man persuade her. After all, she's been getting hungrier and hungrier as the evening goes on. And later, much later, she goes up to a room in Soller's with the blond man. Where else can she go?

At the same time the chauffeur is getting into bed at home beside his wife. His Alpine jacket is hanging ready in the wardrobe. With the letter to the girl in its pocket.

Early on Sunday morning, as soon as she gets up, Kathie goes to Giesing railway station. She's in a hurry, doesn't want to miss any of the trains. She stands right behind the memorial cross.

From there she can see all the passengers, no one can get past her unnoticed. She is waiting for the chauffeur to come along. She waits for every train coming into Giesing station from Perlach, hoping as each train draws in that he will get out of it. Hoping as she hoped yesterday when she never took her eyes off the door at Soller's all evening. Every time a train comes into the station, she imagines him getting out of the carriage. Again and again. The chauffeur. In her mind he's wearing the Alpine jacket. She sees him get out, sees herself calling to him. He would turn to see her, recognize her. Hurry toward her, take her in his arms. She can feel him taking her in his arms. She just has to close her eyes to have him put has arms around her, she even thinks she feels his breath. And there really is a faint breath on her cheek, a draft of air.

"Kathie. What are you doing here?" A voice brings her out of her dreams. She turns in alarm. Wanting it to be his voice, hoping it is. Hoping he's here at last. The voice is so like his, yet without setting eyes on the speaker she knows it can't be him. Feels the disappointment even as she turns, even before she sees who's asking the question. A man she knows in Wolnzach. What's she doing in Munich, he asks, has she found work? And all the rest of it.

Her thoughts are far away, her eyes searching the passengers hurrying past. She has no time to talk to the man from Wolnzach. No time to listen to him telling her he's come to visit his sister in the hospital and so on. Time seems to stand still. He talks and talks. She tries not to lose sight of the train now coming in. Looks at the people passing her. Hardly hears the man from Wolnzach say goodbye. By now she can't bear the waiting anymore. She wants to go out to Waldperlach and the log cabin herself. But suppose he's coming back to Munich at the same time? She can't make up her mind. And what would she be doing out there? He had told her that the log cabin wasn't all his own, his aunt had put some money into the property when he bought it. She didn't want to run into the aunt. What could she say to her? So she stayed where she was. Stayed on the station all day, waiting. Waited all day long.

Twice someone wearing almost the same Alpine jacket as his got out of a train. Both times she ran after the man. Both times it wasn't the chauffeur.

She is discouraged and disappointed, and increasingly uncertain. Just as she is on the point of giving up, because there's no sense in it, she sees him. He is getting out of a train just as she imagined. He's wearing the Alpine jacket in the picture taken outside St. Corbinian's. She recognizes him a long way off. She's about to run to him, throw her arms around him, hold him tight, never let him go again. And then she sees the woman. She's pretty. No older than the chauffeur. She is wearing a dress with a cardigan over it. Her dark blond hair is cut short. They are arm in arm, they seem to know each other very well as they walk past her. Kathie doesn't know whether he has seen her too. She is just behind him when he kisses the woman. Gives her the kiss she wanted for herself. She follows the couple at a distance. Keeping far enough away not to be seen, but near enough to see everything. They go to the trolley stop. Kathie stands at the corner of the street. Waits for them both to get into the trolley, and then she walks all the way back to Soller's in the valley. First with tears running down her cheeks, but after a while they dry up. She walks and walks. Down streets, past buildings, she can't remember where, or how long she has been walking. She remembers only that at some point defiance slowly surfaced in her, and that was what dried her tears at last. She's not going to let this get her down. After all, here she is in Munich, in the big city, come to make her fortune. And she will, too. She's sure of that. She's a pretty girl, after all, as everyone can see. She can see it herself when she passes the display windows. She knows she'll make her fortune. She'll be happy.

*

It's after midnight when the two motorcyclists arrive at Soller's in the valley. They left Nuremberg early in the morning on their NSU bike. They planned to see Munich, go to the Wiesn, stop on the way for a snack, have a nice day. If the motorbike chain hadn't broken outside Ingolstadt they'd have been in Munich by the afternoon. As it was, the two of them pushed the bike to the nearest workshop, and by the time they finally did arrive in Munich it was dark. So they went straight out to the Wiesn, parked the bike, and stayed there until late at night. When they go back for the motorbike they ask the parking attendant where they can find an inn to stay the night. He gives them the name of Soller's in the valley.

At Soller's they ask Gretel the waitress for a room.

No, they don't need two single rooms, they'll share the room and the bed too if necessary. The main thing is somewhere to stay the night.

Oh yes, and they need to be able to park the motorbike safely overnight. Did they have a garage or a shed at Soller's where they could put the NSU?

"You want a room for the night?" asked Gretel.

They weren't choosy, they said, it was only for one night.

Well, there's a room free, she says, but the bed would cost them two marks for the night. Each.

The couple agree, and get her to show them the shed where they can leave the bike. Then they order half-liters of beer from Gretel inside the inn. As they drink their beer one of them tells his friend about the girl who spoke to him just now. While the other man was putting the motorbike in the shed. Just outside their guest-room.

She has asked him whether he'd mind if she spent the night in the room with them, his friend and him. She has nowhere to spend the night, and she was sure Gretel would have asked them about it already.

He was taken by surprise. What could he say? She was pretty, too, so he didn't want to say no. He told his friend to take a quick look in the direction of the bathroom, inconspicuously, and then he could see her. The one in the blue dress, at the table next to the blond man.

No, look the other way, three—no, four tables further on.

He meant the girl with the dark braid of hair, had his friend spotted her now?

The girl with the dark braid of hair glances at them. She is sitting between the blond man and a young woman in a pale coat and a little dark hat.

She raises her glass to them and smiles.

When she passes the two motorcyclists' table later, the one who has been steering the bike gets the impression that she winks at him. The pretext that he must "just go and take a look outside" is all he can think of at this moment, so he follows the girl through the doorway. She is already waiting for him on the other side of the door.

Would it be all right, she asks, for her to spend the night in the room with him and his friend? She doesn't have anywhere else to stay the night.

Yes, that's fine, his friend has already mentioned it, he says. If she likes she can certainly sleep in their room that night. As he talks to her he looks at her face, sees her dark eyes, sees the hair combed back from her forehead and tied into a braid. His friend is right, she's a pretty girl, he likes her.

So as not to just keep staring at her, he asks where she comes from, and what she's doing in Munich. He doesn't care about the answer, he just wants to keep the girl here with him outside the bar for a while. Talk to her about something, anything, just to keep her from going back inside.

She comes from near Ingolstadt, she says, she's looking for a job in Munich.

But she herself doesn't seem interested in a conversation either. Smiles at him. Well, if she could spend the night with him and his friend in their room, she says, then now she'll go back to her acquaintances at the other table. She'll be able to see when the two of them leave the bar and follow them. She stops once more at the door and smiles at him before going back inside. He waits a moment before rejoining his friend at their table.

As soon as the girl is inside their room she undresses without false modesty and without hesitating. She takes off her black patent leather belt, puts it over the chair in the room. Unbuttons the blue dress, puts it down with the best. The two beds, up against the walls, give her just enough room to undress between them. The motorcyclists sit on their beds watching her undress without haste.

They watch her take off her stockings, put them with her dress and belt. In her camisole and underwear, she slips into bed with one of the two men.

He hears the rustle of the bedspread. Smells the warm fragrance of her skin. Closes his eyes as he breathes it in. The girl lets him put both hands under her camisole to push it up, take it off over her head. He passes his hands down her body. Feels her smooth skin, her firm flesh. She lies there perfectly still. He pushes the covers down to the foot of the bed.

He wants to see her, wants to see her naked body.

His hands caress her white breasts. The other man sits on his bed, watching his friend. Sees him take the girl's underwear off as well as her camisole. Sees his friend touch her body with his hands, stroke her legs, feel her vulva. Sees the girl lying naked on the bed. She lies there perfectly still, with her eyes closed.

He watches his friend lie on top of the girl, penetrate her. He sees her naked body glowing faintly white in the darkness of the room. Feels how imagining it all rather than watching it is arousing him. He hears his friend's panting breath when he comes to orgasm. Sees him slip off the girl's body and roll aside.

As if it were the natural thing to do, the girl gets up directly afterward and moves over to him, gets into his bed. Her body is still warm and damp with his friend's sweat; he too touches her body, comes inside her. She lets him do as he likes, lies underneath him soft, warm and still.

In the night the girl changes beds again, gets up as if nothing had happened, goes over to his friend. He sees her lie down beside him, sees his friend's hands on her body again, hears his friend's moaning.

In the morning the girl is back in his bed, sleeping close to him, naked. He sees his friend getting dressed. "I'll wait downstairs for you, join me when you're ready." So saying, his friend closes the door behind him.

Left on his own, he sleeps with her one last time, penetrates the drowsy girl at his side. Feels the soft, warm body under him once more. Then he gets up, gets dressed, and like his friend before him leaves the room

Kathie lay in the bed. Watched the motorcyclist dressing. Picking up garment after garment from the floor: underpants, undershirt, socks, pants. She has pulled the bedspread over her breasts. She had not been ashamed to be there with her breasts uncovered, but she felt cold here in the room at Soller's now. Cold and drained. So she'd pulled the covers up so far up that her bare legs were showing. She lay there rubbing her cold feet together. The motorcyclist had turned to her.

"What is it? Are you cold?"

She just looked briefly at him, without saying a word, without even taking in what he said. She was far away; in her thoughts she was back in the summers of her childhood when she went without shoes and socks. The summers when she ran barefoot along dry, dusty paths, over meadows wet with the morning dew, through puddles with mud between her toes.

She was remembering how her toes were always the smallest and roundest of anyone's, just as she herself had always been the roundest and smallest of them all.

Only when the motorcyclist let the door latch behind him did she come back from her thoughts, was back in bed in the room at Soller's again. Before the motorcyclist left the room he had taken some money out of his jacket pocket. He put it on the bed beside her. On the place next to her feet. She, Kathie, had glanced briefly up at him and looked at him without seeing him.

Once the door had closed Kathie got up too. She pushed the warm bedspread aside. Stood up, put on the clothes still hanging over the chair from the day before, picked up the money.

She could wash at Mitzi's. She wanted to be out of that room. Go through the city, cross the Viktualienmarkt to Mariahilfplatz.

The motorcyclists were still in the yard of the inn, standing beside their bike and looking awkward. One of them tried to start a conversation with her. What was she going to do now? Where was she going?

Kathie didn't answer. What could she have told him—that she herself didn't know what she was going to do today, didn't know where she was going? What use would that have been? Or should she have told them about the summers when she went bare-legged, and the lovely time she had wading through puddles with her bare feet? Should she have told him that those summers were the best in her life, and this morning, when she had watched one of the two of them dressing, she had guessed—no, she had known—that they would always be the best summers in her entire life?

Or should she have told them about the brilliant red of the cotton reel in her hand? A red that warmed her, like the brief happiness she had felt out there with the chauffeur that afternoon. What good would that have done her? She didn't want to reply, so she said nothing. Just shrugged her shoulders briefly and walked away.

She went toward Mariahilfplatz, the way she had gone with the chauffeur, an eternity ago. It was only a couple of days in the past, yet it seemed like a lifetime since then. She passed the market women's stalls. Went along Reichenbachstrasse and over the Reichenbach Bridge. She stopped for a moment on the bridge at the place where the chauffeur had kissed her. Went on to Mariahilfplatz. Her head was empty, no thoughts in it at all.

Mitzi opened the door wearing only her underclothes. She sat opposite Kathie at the kitchen table in her camisole. She pushed a mug of coffee over to Kathie. Kathie put both hands around the mug. Drew it closer to her and felt the warmth in her clammy fingers.

Later, Kathie took the motorcyclists' money out of her bag and put it on the table. She got off the chair and went over to the sofa. Just as she was, she lay down on the sofa and fell asleep.

Sometime during the day Mitzi left the apartment, because when Kathie got up again she was alone. She stood up, washed her face and hands and between her legs. Dressed, put her little blue hat on, slipped into her green coat, and went out.

KATHIE

Tuesday October 13 was a mild autumn day. The leaves on the trees and bushes had already turned russet brown. Johann Reiss rode his motorbike out along the highroad toward Hohenschäftlarn with his brother Alwin in the side-car. They had set out early. The autumnal mist was just beginning to lift, the sun could already be seen here and there. It was going to be a fine day. One of the last days of late summer weather this year. They had left Munich behind them. There was hardly any traffic on the road. They both felt it was pleasant to go out for the day, riding along with no particular destination in mind, stopping for a snack, riding on, enjoying the landscape. They had all the time in the world today.

They rode out of Hohenschäftlarn, past the abbey, and on in the direction of Säge. Just after the Bruckenfischer inn they turned off the main road. Took the little road going south. It was only a path really, not a paved road. Johann reduced speed, avoiding the potholes. They went on through fields and meadows, down to the old millstream.

They both knew this area, they often rode out here. On almost all their days off. They came to bathe in the millstream in summer, and in autumn to pick blackberries or look for mushrooms, or just to spend a day out. Their way took them a little way upstream along the course of the millstream. Now they decided to stop for a break, sit on the banks of the stream, get some rest, just do as they liked.

The banks of the old millstream were densely overgrown with reeds and bushes. On both sides of the stream and up the slope. Here and there narrow tracks led from the path down to the stream, to secret places for anglers, bathers, pairs of lovers. They rode on past those because they wanted to get to the old bridge, the only place where you could sit directly on the slope by the stream, which was not overgrown there. There'd been nothing left of the bridge itself for a long time now. You could see the remains of it only in the water near the bank, where the old foundations, even though they were just a few stones, kept the vegetation from spreading. It was the one place where you had a clear view of the bank and could climb down to the stream. They were planning to get off the bike and lie on a rug in the sun. They had brought a thermos flask and sandwiches, and afterward they would go on along the stream and pick mushrooms for their mother on the way back, as they'd promised her.

Now they have reached the place and left the motorbike. Johann goes a little way down the slope toward the stream. Then he sees the little blue hat. More of a cap really, dark blue with pale trimmings. A ribbon bow, white ribbons drifting from it in the slowly flowing water. The cap itself is caught, stuck on a piece of wood, flotsam that has ended up beside the left-hand bank of the stream, among the twigs and soil washed up there.

All he notices are the ribbons drifting in the water. The dancing white ribbons on the cap. Feeling curious, he goes closer for a better view. He climbs a little way down the slope until he can see the hat clearly. He looks at it in surprise, wondering whether to fish it out of the water, this little hat dancing on the current, and if so how. His eyes wander along the bank, but he can't see any good place to climb in. He decides to try further up, climb down to the water there, wade out to the cap and retrieve it. It won't be going anywhere in the meantime. It will stay where it is; the current is weak.

He walks a few paces upstream, turns up his trouser-legs, takes off his shoes. Climbs down to the edge of the bank. Leans forward to see if he's reached the little ford. No, not yet, the bank drops more steeply at this point, the water looks to him deeper than it was near the cap. His glance wanders further along the bank. The root-stock of a tree catches his eye. There's something white underneath it.

Then he sees her. She is lying wedged under that root-stock in the water. Only the white skin of her legs sticking out from under the roots is in view. The rest is out of sight.

He calls for his brother, who comes, reluctantly. Doesn't believe what Johann called out to him. "You're seeing spooks. Where is this girl in the water?"

"Here, I can see her. Hang on to me, will you? The bank's too steep here. You'll have to hold me so I don't fall in."

Johann holds his arm out to his brother, who takes it and holds Johann firmly, bracing himself against his weight. Johann leans out as far as he can over the millstream. Looks into the deep, clear, slowly flowing water. All he can see of the body is one hand and the legs.

The hand is lying to the side of the body. There's something gleaming silver on the wrist. A bracelet. No, a piece of wire tying it up.

"What is it?" Alwin asks. "What's happened? What can you see?"

"Not much," says his brother. "It's a woman, or a girl. She must be lying face down. She's covered with spruce branches. I can't see anything except her legs and one hand."

"Let me try—maybe I can see more," says Alwin.

Johann looks for a better foothold on the bank. Cautiously, Alwin relaxes his grasp and slides down the slope too. Tries to see the girl, leans out from the bank, always taking care not to slide down it. Then he can see her too, her bare legs in the water, the glittering wire around her wrist. The wire tying the spruce branches to her body. Only now does he believe his brother, now that he sees it with his own eyes.

It is several hours before they come back with the police. They have been home to Munich, and once there they went to the police station and reported finding the dead woman.

"Why not at the scene of the crime?" the officer on duty asked them. "Why didn't you go straight to the police in Schäftlarn?"

The brothers don't know. They say nothing. They just wanted to get well away from what they'd found. They'd packed up their things in a hurry, Alwin tells the officer, and then Johann rode all the way home.

They just hadn't thought of reporting their find to the police in Schäftlarn. It simply didn't occur to them. Because that woman, or maybe she was a girl, had been murdered.

How did they know that? How could they be so sure the person they found was a crime victim?

The wire, she was tied up with wire. They'd both seen the wire around her legs and her hand. They'd seen it clearly.

Of course they were prepared to show the police the way. And so now, hours later, they are back in the same place for the second time that day. On this occasion in a Munich police car. They show the senior officer with them where she is. The dead girl. Wedged under the root-stock, covered with branches. One of the policemen tries moving the branches on the dead girl's back. He pushes at the body with a long stick. The branches stay put, they won't be shifted. He tries again. Tries to fish the entire body out from under the root-stock. He keeps pushing it with the stick, but neither the body nor the branches will budge.

Only next day, when the police have finally got the girl out of the water, will they see why. They discover that the branches had been tied around her body with wire. Wrapped around it. Underneath the branches are the dead girl's dress and coat, done up in a bundle and, like the branches themselves, lashed to her body with wire. They will find the stone that was supposed to keep the body from floating to the surface; it drops back into the water as they take the dead girl out. They will find her shoes, carried away by the current, not very far downstream but a little way from the body, like her hat.

One officer will move the branches away from her face and torso. He will see the face of a girl about twenty years old at the most. Her eye color is brown, her eyelids only half closed in death. She has a short, snub nose. The full lips of her mouth are closed. He will see the dead girl's dark brown hair tied into a braid and hanging over her shoulder, falling almost down to her waist.

She is not tall, rather small and stocky. Her torn upper garments show her bare breasts.

They will take the dead girl out of the water and up the slope of the bank, and then lay her down on the grass. They will photograph her, and the pictures will show her lying there half-dressed, her stockings torn off, no underwear. They will show the abrasions and bruises on her skin. Her torn, broken fingernails. The marks of strangulation. She is still wearing a little bead necklace. Worthless. It will fall off her and come apart only as they lay her in a lead coffin and take her to forensics. The beads will drop on the grass and lie there.

*

I live in Lothringerstrasse in Munich. I lodge in a small room there. It's big enough for me, and now that I'm out of work I'm thankful that I can afford it at all. The unemployment benefit isn't much, and times are hard. My landlady Frau Lederer is a widow. She told me her husband was with the post office. Her pension is only small, so she rents a room to a lodger.

Yesterday morning, she asked me if I'd look after her cousin Frau Hertl from Wolnzach, because Frau Hertl doesn't know her way around Munich very well, and I'd probably have time now that I'm out of work. "You'd be doing me a great favor, Herr Feichtinger."

Frau Hertl was going to search for her daughter, my landlady said. The girl was here in Munich. She'd come to look for a job, like so many young girls, and she hadn't sent any word home since arriving. Her mother was worried, so she was coming to Munich to try to find her. I said I'd be happy to help her look for the girl. I had no other plans that day.

Frau Hertl arrived at Frau Lederer's apartment at nine-thirty in the morning. It was Wednesday October 14, 1931. She'd come straight from the station, she told me later.

She and Frau Lederer talked for a little while in the apartment. I wasn't present, they were both sitting at the kitchen table. When I came in they stopped talking, and Frau Lederer introduced me to Frau Hertl. I didn't want to stand around, so I said that if she didn't mind we'd start at once. That was fine

for Frau Hertl, and so we set off together. I was carrying a case
that Frau Lederer had given her cousin. The girl Kathie had left
it with her, and never came back for it. So we went off together.
I asked her where she would like to go first.

"To Number 13 Ickstattstrasse." She wanted to call on a
Frau Bösl there. She'd heard that her daughter had been at
Ickstattstrasse, she said. Frau Bösl knew Kathie from the hop-
picking. She came to Wolnzach every year to pick hops.

So I took her to the address she'd given me. A lady with a
small child opened the door. I assume it was Frau Bösl, because
there wasn't anyone else in the apartment and that was the
name on the plate by the door. She took us into the kitchen.
Frau Hertl and me. I didn't want to be nosy, so I stayed in
the background.

Frau Hertl asked right away if her daughter Kathie had been
here in Ickstattstrasse, and whether Frau Bösl had any idea
where she was now. Yes, she'd been here, young Kathie had.
But only for two days. She'd been looking for a job in those two
days, but she hadn't found anything. It was very hard to find a
job these days. And then Kathie had moved in with an acquaintance of hers. She couldn't have stayed here any longer, not in
this little apartment.

The child sat on Frau Bösl's lap all the time she was talking
to Frau Hertl, munching a piece of brown bread and staring
at the strange lady. What was the name of Frau Bösl's acquaintance, Frau Hertl asked, and where could she find her?

The acquaintance's name was Mitzi Zimmermann. "Mitzi
lives in Mariahilfplatz. Number 29. But you could always ask
in Gruftstrasse too. Near the arch. I don't know what number."
Because the woman who lives in Gruftstrasse goes to Wolnzach
for the hop-picking every year too. Perhaps she knows Kathie,
says Frau Bösl, and then perhaps can tell us her whereabouts.

"She could have gone there." But there was no point in going to Gruftstrasse before evening, because the woman was out all day.

So Frau Hertl thanked Frau Bösl and asked if she owed her anything for giving Kathie board and lodging in her apartment for two days. But Frau Bösl waved that aside and said it was all right.

When there was no more to discuss, we stood up and said goodbye. We were on the stairs when Frau Bösl came after us. "Kathie left her umbrella with me, and she didn't come back for it." She gave Frau Hertl the umbrella, and before she could say any more Frau Bösl ran back into her apartment because the child in there had begun crying. Frau Hertl went downstairs carrying the umbrella, and I followed her. Then we went on to Mariahilfplatz and Mitzi Zimmermann.

We found Mitzi Zimmermann in her apartment. She wasn't alone, there was a man in the apartment too. I think he was Mitzi's husband, but I don't know, because he didn't introduce himself. He seemed very much at home there in Mitzi's place. Then we sat on the sofa in the kitchen living room, Frau Hertl and I. With Mitzi and the man opposite us. He was very dark-haired, and he did all the talking. Mitzi sat beside him and said hardly anything. Yes, said the black-haired man, Kathie had stayed here for two days. "Until Saturday evening. Then she left. She said she was going to a relation in Pasing. It was Pasing she said, wasn't it?" He nudged Mitzi Zimmermann, dug his elbow into her ribs, and she nodded and agreed, "Yes, Pasing, that's what she said."

Frau Hertl couldn't believe it, because they had no relatives in Pasing, nowhere Kathie could have gone. "There aren't any Hertls in Munich except in Denning. None in Pasing. Did Kathie really say Pasing?"

Mitzi Zimmermann discussed it with the black-haired man and after a while they agreed yes, it could have been Denning, but they couldn't be sure of it. After that Mitzi Zimmermann just sat there in silence again.

Frau Hertl said she had the address of the Denning Hertls in her handbag, and couldn't Mitzi or the gentleman tell her any more about her daughter? Who she had been mixing with, where had she been going while she stayed here with them? After all, she'd stayed there for two days, she must have said something about it. "Or perhaps you saw my Kathie with someone?" They couldn't give her any name or address to help her further.

They'd seen her necking with a fellow, a chauffeur he was. She was wild about him. From what he'd seen, said the black-haired man, he'd guess there was something going on between them. "It'd be a shame if the girl fell into the wrong hands. She's a pretty girl, there's many a pretty girl has come to grief before now."

Frau Hertl asked Mitzi whether Kathie might be with this chauffeur, and did she know his name and address? She begged her to help her find her daughter. Mitzi Zimmermann only swore. "Good Christ, how in hell would I know the address?"

Frau Hertl wasn't giving up, she asked her again and again. Maybe Kathie really had told Mitzi Zimmermann more in the two days she stayed with them, and they just couldn't remember it. Please would they think again? She was so worried about her daughter.

"There's nothing more to talk about. Kathie wasn't here long, and she didn't tell us anything. I didn't ask any questions either. I really can't help you." There was only Kathie's little black handbag, she'd left that here, Mitzi had only just remembered it. She got up and went into the next room. It would be on the window sill just where Kathie left it, she said.

Mitzi Zimmermann gave the handbag to Frau Hertl, who opened it and looked inside at once. She was very surprised, because Kathie's belt was in the handbag. The belt that went with her dress. Apart from her belt there were only a couple of scraps of paper in the bag. Nothing to help us any further.

Even as she left, Frau Hertl turned to Mitzi and impressed it on her that if the child, if her Kathie came back, she should go to Frau Lederer, and she would get money there for the journey home. She had seen to that. Mitzi mustn't forget. She was to tell Kathie to come back home.

Then we went on from Mariahilfplatz to the trolley stop in Ludwigstrasse. The poor woman seemed very downcast. I felt so sorry for her, I didn't know what to do, how to comfort her. On the way to the trolley stop she told me she thought her daughter had been to an inn. An acquaintance from Wolnzach had heard she'd been seen there and told her about it. The place was known as Soller's, and she'd like to go to it. She didn't want to leave any stone unturned. Did I know where the inn was, and had I ever been to it myself?

So I went to Soller's with her. First we looked in at the Metzgerbräu beer cellar. Kathie's mother asked about her there too, but we didn't find her or anyone who could help us.

We had no luck at Soller's either. No one there had seen Kathie.

Now we didn't know where else to look for Kathie, so we went to the Grüner Hof inn. Frau Hertl had left her luggage there, and we left her daughter's case full of clothes, which we'd been carrying around with us all this time. We left the umbrella and the handbag there too. Then we went to the railway station.

Frau Hertl said the man she knew in Wolnzach had also told her that he'd seen Kathie here at the station last Sunday, and she seemed to be waiting for every train coming in. Kathie must have been there almost all day, because Frau Hertl's friend had seen her when he arrived, and then later, when he took the train home, she was still there.

On the way to the station Frau Hertl said she had to do a little shopping here in Munich. Could I go with her, she asked, so that she wouldn't be all alone? She didn't want to on her own. So I went with her.

I accompanied her from the station to Paul-Heyse-Strasse. Frau Hertl went into a draper's shop there. Hofmann is the name of the business. She wanted to buy some dress material. I waited for her outside the shop. After about half an hour she came out again, and said the woman in the shop had told her Kathie had been there, and Frau Hofmann thought Kathie was working as a maid for a lawyer now. She, Frau Hofmann, had given Kathie the address herself. The lawyer's wife was a good customer of hers. So Frau Hertl was sure that the girl who went into the shop was Kathie. The Hertl family had been buying fabric from the Hofmann shop for years, and the girl had mentioned her name too. That gave Frau Hertl hope, and Frau Hofmann had been kind enough to telephone the lawyer and ask after Kathie. But she'd never been there.

Then I went back to the Grüner Hof with Frau Hertl. We took the dress material she had bought there, and put it with the rest of her luggage. After that I went with her to the police station that deals with such things, and she reported Kathie missing.

I can't say any more. I've already told you all I can remember.

*

The passerby, a woman, will tell the police later that the girl was standing with her back to the rotunda grating. She was looking in the direction of Sonnenstrasse. She, the passerby herself, was standing at the trolley stop. First she didn't notice the girl at all. Only when she heard her voice did she notice, and look her way.

"I've only been in Munich for a week."

The girl was small, slightly plump. Sixteen or maybe eighteen years old, wearing a green coat. Later, the woman would recognize the coat at once, at the police station.

"I'm not going with you. I don't want to."

The girl's hat, more of a cap really, didn't hide her face. There was something pale around the hat, maybe a ribbon. The passerby couldn't tell in the light from the street lamp; the couple was standing outside the place where it fell. But she was able to say, later, that there had been something light around the girl's face. However, she couldn't confirm with complete certainty that the hat they showed her was the one the girl had been wearing.

"I'm new here. I don't know my way around."

The man leaned a little way over to the girl as he talked to her, in a muted voice that no one else could hear. You could guess at what he was saying only from the way he moved and held himself.

Curious now, the passerby watched the couple. The man was twenty-five, maybe younger. "He was dressed like a chauffeur, pants stopping just above the ankle, dark socks, a leather jacket, the kind of thing drivers wear."

The girl's voice dropped too. The passerby heard only a little laugh. When the trolley came she got on it. As she boarded the trolley, she looked at the couple.

The girl had taken the man's arm. They were walking quickly toward the hospital complex. The woman watched until she lost sight of them.

(Interrogation of Josef Kalteis, continued)

—What do I like to do best? I like cycling around. I look
at the countryside. And the women too, of course.

—Yes, I like women. What kind of a man would I be if I
didn't look at them?

—If I haven't been out of doors in a long time I can't
stand it no more. I have to get out, I have to walk
around, or even better ride my bike. I get quite worked
up then, all restless. Everything seems so cramped, I
have to get out of doors.

—Well, then I ride my bike around and look at the
women. I like brunettes best, smart brunettes. And
I like a nice fat ass. I don't like them too thin. No, I
don't like Skinny Lizzies at all. What does a girl need
to have? Nice knockers, yes, but a good ass even more
than nice knockers. So's you've got a good handful to
hold on to.

—When you're cycling, well, all the women are coming your way. Their skirts keep riding up as they cycle
along. Then you can see their undies. I like that, nothing
wrong with that, is there? They do it on purpose. They
dress for cycling specially so their skirts will ride up
and anyone can see their undies. Their undies and the
way their thighs rub together, that gets me all worked
up. But that's what they want, they want it. You take
my word, they want you to grab them good and hard.
They like it, that's what women want.

—Sometimes I follow one on my bike. Look at her ass
rubbing back and forth on the saddle, think how it'd be
if she was sitting on top of me. Rubbing back and forth
on me.

—Just cuddling and that, no, it don't do anything for me, I like a girl to fight back, twist and turn. It's only when I have to hold her good and hard with all my strength I really like it. Having to grab her and hold her there. That's what women want.

—My wife, she don't really enjoy it till it gets a bit rough. They want to be a bit scared, that's what makes it fun. You take my word for it.

(The public prosecutor places a brown cardboard box on the table in front of Kalteis. He takes a photograph out of the box.)

—*I never seen that girl.*

—Why are you showing me this photo? Why put the girl's picture in front of me? I never seen the girl in my life. I can't remember this girl.

—What do you mean, some woman saw me with the girl? Well, could be I saw her once. Let's have another look at the photo. What did you say she's called? Hertl? I can't remember.

—Yes, could be I once met a girl at the Oktoberfest what looked something like this. What's her first name, then? Kathie?

—You can always meet girls on the Wiesn. Maybe I did once meet a Kathie on the Wiesn.

—Okay, I admit I knew the girl. I met her at the Oktoberfest.

—She was standing by the roundabout. Smiled at me. I liked her right away. So I went over to her and talked to her. Then we went on the chairoplane together and the ghost train. I put my arm around her in the ghost train.

She didn't mind. She went along with me right away,
she was willing. That's how it seemed to me, she liked
it. After a while I asked if she liked nature, if she'd go
out with me, somewhere out of Munich.

—I don't remember when, not now. I think it was still
early when I asked her. Can't remember now.

—We left the Wiesn, we went for a walk. Went through
the city. I don't know all the streets by name, can't tell
you exactly where. We went to Thalkirchen.

—Then she wanted a cuddle while we was walking. That
don't interest me much, to be honest, cuddling a girl. I
don't get nothing out of it. Never did interest me. But
I went along with her just because I wanted to have it
off with her.

—I wanted to have it off, that's why we went further out.

—Nothing wrong with that, is there? Nothing wrong
with meeting a girl at the Oktoberfest and going out
of town to have it off with her. What's the matter
with that?

—The girl knew what I wanted or she wouldn't have
come with me. We cuddled a bit because that's what she
liked. Yes, then I grabbed her a bit harder. That's what I
like myself, and she liked it too.

—That's what spices it up for me, it has to be a bit
rough, a bit of violence in it. If the girl goes all coy, if
she resists . . .

—She liked it, she went along with me. Went along with
me fucking her. Afterward I'll have taken her back to
Munich. What else would I have done?

(The public prosecutor puts newspaper cuttings
about the murder of Katharina Hertl in front of

Kalteis. Newspaper cuttings found in the suspect's apartment.)

—*What's this about? I kept those newspaper stories because I knew the girl. And then you read next day about how she's dead. You keep these things, that's only natural. Anyone would do it, bet you'd do it too!*
—Why didn't I say what I knew? Can't remember no more. I guess I was scared you'd pin it on me.

(The public prosecutor places a mummified piece of tissue with hair on it in front of Kalteis. It was found with the newspaper story and other such finds in an old stove in the suspect's loft.)

—*What's that? What's that supposed to be?*
—I've no idea what it is.

(The public prosecutor tells Kalteis that on forensic examination the find has proved to be part of a vulva with the pubic hair still on it. According to the forensic investigators, the mummified piece of tissue can be related to a series of other such finds taken from dead women. In addition, Kalteis's fingerprints are on the container in which the item was found.)

—*Where did you get all this? What's this all about?*

(Kalteis looks incredulously at the finds. The public prosecutor describes precisely where they were found, in an old disused stove in the loft belonging to Kalteis's apartment. The public prosecutor goes on to ask the suspect why he cut the girl's vulva out while she was still alive.)

—*I never did! That's a lie! She was dead! Dead! Listen, she was dead!*
—Listen, will you help me if I tell you everything? Will you help me? It wasn't me, it's something driving me. I can't do nothing about it, it makes me do things, I have to go out, I have to find something . . . I can't resist it. Will you help me?
—I went out with that girl. She just cuddled. That don't do a thing for me.
—I didn't feel nothing. So I took her where we wouldn't be disturbed. Out there you can go uphill and downhill, there's plenty of places you can be alone.
—That's why I took her out there. Then I grabbed hold of her, tore her underwear off. I knocked her down and tore her underwear off. I held her by the throat with one hand.
—She fought back, but that's what she wanted, I mean, she went out there with me.
—All I remember is, I knocked her down and stuck it in her.
—She didn't move no more after that. Didn't move. She lay there, she didn't move. I guess I'd held my hand too hard around her throat. She didn't move.
—It was the first one died on me. I wasn't myself when I grabbed her. It wasn't till after I'd come I noticed she wasn't moving no more. I was trembling all over, because she just lay there, wasn't moving no more. I was so worked up, she'd fought back so hard, that

really got me going, I was beside myself. The whole thing was really good . . .

—I can't remember what happened afterward, not now. I wanted to clear her away so as nobody would find her. Clear her out of the way.

—I went to the old millstream. It was kind of a branch of the old millstream. I tied her hands and feet together. I threw her in. I tied a stone to her too, so she'd sink. Then I went back to Munich, I don't remember what I did then.

—Where did I get the wire? I had it in my pocket. Why did I put it in my pocket? I don't remember no more.

—Afterward I had a funny feeling. Kind of a tingling. I couldn't get no rest. What did I do with her before I put her in the water? I can't remember.

—Only that I wasn't myself. I felt a little ashamed. Because she'd died in my hands, but after a while I wanted it again. Wanted that feeling again.

—I always had that funny feeling afterward, I wanted it again. That's why I cut her cunt out too and took it with me, because I wanted that feeling again.

—I wanted it again and again, I was in such a state, I wasn't myself no more, I always felt ashamed afterward, but after a while that was all forgotten and I was at it again. Like a wild animal, that's what it feels like, I was at it again . . . again and again.